THE MAZE

BOOKS BY WILL HOBBS

THE MAZE

Will Hobbs

Morrow Junior Books
New York

Published by Morrow Junior Books
a division of William Morrow and Company, Inc.
1350 Avenue of the Americas, New York, NY 10019
www.williammorrow.com

Printed in the United States of America.

10   9   8   7

Library of Congress Cataloging-in-Publication Data
Hobbs, Will.
The maze/Will Hobbs.
p. cm.
Summary: Rick, a fourteen-year-old foster child, escapes from a juvenile
detention facility near Las Vegas and travels to Canyonlands National
Park in Utah, where he meets a bird biologist working on a project to
reintroduce condors to the wild.
ISBN 0-688-15092-6
[1. Runaways—Fiction.   2. Foster home care—Fiction.   3. Condors—
Fiction.   4. Endangered species—Fiction.   5. Wildlife conservation—
Fiction.   6. Canyonlands National Park (Utah)—Fiction.]   I. Title.
PZ7.H6524Map 1998   [Fic]—dc21   98-10791   CIP AC

to Derek James

*whose luminous cover paintings
invite readers into my stories*

MAZE DISTRICT

CANYONLANDS NATIONAL PARK
UTAH

1

Rick Walker tried to swallow, but his mouth was too dry.

"The state of Nevada has a problem with you . . ." the judge began, then paused to glare at him over his reading glasses.

Rick Walker glanced at his social worker, seated beside him on his right. He wondered if the pause meant he was supposed to answer. He wasn't sure what to make of this bald and bony-headed old man who was the judge. The sign on the door of his courtroom said he was THE HONORABLE SAMUEL L. BENDIX. At the moment he seemed more hostile than honorable.

"Why?" the judge suddenly demanded.

Rick was confused. Why what? What was the judge asking him? Once again his eyes went to his social worker for help. Janice Baker seemed confused too.

As Rick looked back toward the black robe, he felt his lip quiver. In an instant he forgot that his social worker had warned him about the judge's "enormous discretionary power." He reverted to his instincts for dealing with powerful adversaries: don't show fear, or you'll be eaten alive.

With a slight shrug he asked, "Why what?"

He saw the judge's skin flush red up and over his skull. "Why were you throwing the stones, repeatedly, at the stop sign? Why would anyone throw more than thirty rocks at a stop sign?"

Rick knew he couldn't afford to say anything further that would get taken the wrong way. He hesitated, looking deep inside for the real answer. That's what the judge wanted: the real answer.

His hesitation lengthened. Rick didn't know the real answer. The only thing he could think of was his grandmother dying. Everything that went wrong happened because of that. But the judge wasn't going to accept excuses, especially something that happened four years ago. Why *was* he throwing those rocks?

He didn't know the answer himself. It was all too confusing. All he could remember was being in a sort of trance. It had happened only a few blocks from the group home, on his way from school. He didn't know he had thrown so many rocks. He couldn't even remember what he'd been thinking about. "I don't know," he said at last.

"You *don't know* . . ." the judge repeated incredulously.

Rick tried his best. "It wasn't for any specific reason," he explained.

"Not for any reason."

The rising cadence of the judge's voice felt ominous. Rick unfolded his arms and put them down by his sides. "Just general frustration, I guess," he managed.

The judge looked aside, put his fist to his chin, looked back at Rick. "*General frustration* is what I'm feeling right now myself," the judge said. "Just this morning, over coffee, I read about two juveniles no older than you bludgeoning a nine-year-old to death with a baseball bat."

So? Rick thought. What does that have to do with me?

The judge paused. His eyes had drifted, unfocusing, to the floor. "So many with no conscience," he said as if to himself. "A petty offender one day becomes a murderer the next. It didn't used to be like this."

The judge's eyes were suddenly back in focus and locked on Rick. "Didn't I tell you just six weeks ago that I didn't want to see you in my courtroom ever again?"

"Yes," Rick agreed.

"Yes, *Your Honor*," his social worker said under her breath.

"Yes, Your Honor."

Rick felt so light-headed he thought he might faint. In the corner of his vision he was aware of a man in a police uniform coming up the side aisle. It was young Mike Brown, his probation officer, with his trim dark mustache and his face blank like a robot's.

"Say you're sorry," Janice Baker whispered.

Rick glanced at her. He should have said it himself, before this. Now the judge was glaring worse than ever, knowing he'd just been instructed to say he was sorry.

He couldn't, not now. Not when he was being forced to. He had a certain amount of pride. What could the judge do to him anyway? Janice Baker had told him about a place near Lake Tahoe for kids like him who'd gotten into a little bit of trouble. It didn't sound so bad, being in the pine trees and the mountains. It couldn't be much worse than the group home he was in now in Reno. The couple running the group home was only doing it for the money. They didn't even care enough to come to court with him.

His social worker appealed to Rick with a glance. He shook his head.

With a disapproving look at him, Janice Baker rose to her feet. "Please take into account, Your Honor, Rick's background. He's only fourteen. In the last four years, he has lived in foster homes in Fresno, Stockton, Merced, and Sacramento, California, as well as a foster home and a group home here in Reno. During that time he has been enrolled in six different schools. He has never known either of his parents. He was raised by his grandmother, who died when he was ten, leaving him an orphan, completely alone in the world."

Rick recoiled at the word *orphan*. He hated that word, hated that it even existed. He didn't think people should use it. It made him sound pitiful.

The judge peered over his glasses. "His file is right in front of my eyes, Miss Baker."

She paused. "Of course, Your Honor."

"If you will, Officer Brown," the judge instructed.

The probation officer cleared his throat. "I've visited Rick three times at the group home," he began. "At present I have five kids to check in on there. I've known Rick for only six weeks. Haven't got him to talk much. Don't have much of a feel for him."

"I understand, Officer Brown. So many of them seem to be bundles of attitude with no substance inside, nothing they really care about. No conscience, no remorse."

Rick wondered if he should say something. Now was the time to at least say he was sorry.

But he wasn't sorry, not really. It was a stupid thing he had done, but it wasn't as if he'd killed somebody. Now it came back to him, how he felt when he was throwing the stones. He was angry. He was angry about ending up in the group home after all his bad luck with the foster homes. He was still angry that his mother hadn't had the character to at least come and meet him after his grandmother died, that he'd never had so much as a photograph to help him form an image of his father.

The judge stared at him again. "Who is Rick Walker?" the judge intoned. "That is the question."

Am I supposed to answer this? Rick wondered. What kind of question is this?

"Answer the question," the judge demanded.

Rick thought hard. Again he was swimming in confusion. Deep down, he didn't really *know* who he was. He hadn't for a long time. And he was angry about that too. That was why he couldn't say he was sorry. It's impossible to say you're sorry, and mean it, when you're angry. He didn't deserve all that had happened to him.

Or did he?

He didn't know the answer to that either. Why was he always being bumped along? Why was it he'd never been adopted?

"Rick Walker is just somebody trying to get by," he managed awkwardly.

The judge shook his head, put his knuckles back to his chin.

Rick knew he wasn't dangerous to anybody, if that

was what the judge was getting at. Throwing rocks at a stop sign wouldn't suggest that he was, would it? He'd never hurt anybody.

"For violating the express conditions of your probation, six months in Blue Canyon Youth Detention Center," the judge pronounced.

Rick's social worker gasped. "Your Honor!" she blurted out.

Rick went instantly numb. Paralyzed. Struck by lightning. He'd heard about Blue Canyon, down near Las Vegas. There were even murderers in there. He looked frantically around his social worker to Mike Brown. The probation officer was surprised too.

"His only prior offense was shoplifting," Rick heard his social worker saying. "Two CDs." Her voice sounded far away suddenly. "Isn't there a no-security facility in the woods near Lake Tahoe, Your Honor, that would be more appropriate?"

"Thought of that," the judge snapped. "The school there is not accredited. This young man's aptitude tests indicate strong academic potential. Much better school program at Blue Canyon."

The red-faced judge turned his merciless eyes on Rick once again. "Maybe this time I can make an impression on you, young man. Serve your six months, stay out of trouble, and don't let me see you in my courtroom again."

2

Four and a half months into Rick's sentence/ there
were still mornings like this one, when the 5:30 A.M.
wake-up alarm took him utterly by surprise.

As quickly as he realized where he was, he
swiveled his legs to the floor. Lagging in bed brought
trouble. The first thing he saw was jackal-faced Mr.
Northcut, his unit's "youth leader," as the guards were
called, standing back against the wall and studying
him with that habitual look of scornful amusement.

With a twinge of regret Rick remembered telling
his Blue Canyon social worker, two weeks earlier, that
he'd seen the guard from the next unit take cash from
one of the maintenance men. Could the guards,
including Northcut, possibly know he'd told?

He couldn't let himself get paranoid. His social
worker had promised he wouldn't reveal his source.

Now Rick was awake enough to remember why he was worried. His social worker had been fired yesterday. There was plenty of reason to worry.

It was the last day of September. Blue Canyon was on a week's break between school sessions. Breaks were inherently unstable and dangerous. He would lift weights for an hour in the gym and spend the rest of the time in the library—those were the only two places he felt safe. Those were the places where people minded their own business. In the weight section of the gym even the most aggressive guys focused on themselves, not on anyone else. The library was intolerably boring unless you were actually going to read. And guys who liked to read weren't the kind looking for trouble.

Hanging out in the TV room—that was entirely different. Guys blurted things out at the TV, at each other. People got offended very easily. Fights started over nothing and got bloody fast.

Rick filled his breakfast tray with pancakes, sausage, toast, and orange juice, then looked for an empty table. He didn't have allies to eat with. Allies meant obligations to help carry out illegal schemes. His strategy for getting out of Blue Canyon on time and in one piece was to go it alone. Building up his body signaled it was obvious he would fight if he had to. He kept his mouth shut and generally lay low. So far only one guy had picked a fight with him. Rick had surprised himself with his own ferocity. It was over in a few seconds, and nothing had come of it.

Rick spotted a table with only one person at it, the Kid Who Eats Glass. The boy's real name was Killian. Rick sat down at the other end of the table. He knew he wouldn't have to have a conversation with Killian.

They saw each other in the library almost every day, but Killian was accustomed to talking only with himself.

Killian didn't like to read the books; he liked to eat them. This morning he was carrying around a half-eaten issue of *Reader's Digest*. Killian's literary appetite was a source of good-natured amusement for the librarian, Mr. Bramwell, who had the kids call him Mr. B. "That's what librarians live for, Rick!" Mr. B. had once proclaimed. "Patrons who devour books!"

Rick felt sorry for the boy with the gaunt face and bad teeth. He had asked Mr. B. once if he knew how Killian had gotten so messed up. It wasn't something Rick would have asked another kid. Among the kids the whole subject of backgrounds was much too embarrassing, too explosive.

"Killian's almost too sad to talk about," the librarian replied. "His parents literally treated him like a dog. Kept him chained in their backyard, made him live in a doghouse. Fed him out of a dog dish."

To Rick this seemed too monstrous to comprehend. "Were they foster parents or what?"

"No, his natural parents."

Rick had said nothing. He would have to think about this. Compared with this, he had been lucky to have been abandoned by his parents to his grandmother.

Mr. B. was reading his mind. "You had your grandmother," the librarian said. "That's why you turned out okay."

"Turned out okay?" Rick repeated sardonically. "Look where I am, Mr. B."

"You'll do okay, Rick. You'll do okay. I have faith in you. Heck, you're normal!"

It meant the world when Mr. B. had said that.

A sudden clatter of dishes brought Rick back to his half-eaten pancakes. He hadn't realized that Killian had gotten up and left. He finished quickly, then went straight to the gym. Some guys would come to shoot baskets, but the weight corner would be practically empty. Most guys wouldn't work out early or on full stomachs.

There was talk that the weights were going to be removed soon. Some people probably thought that a detention center shouldn't be helping criminals become stronger criminals, but he didn't agree. When guys knew they were strong, they weren't so preoccupied about having to fight. They knew that if it came to it, they could stick up for themselves, so they didn't go around with such aggressive attitudes.

He pushed himself through the workout with a few more repetitions than ever before. His body had toughened like steel. Whenever he looked in the mirror at his armor he surprised himself. He looked like a stranger in more ways than one. He'd almost forgotten how to smile; the boy in the mirror looked wary even of himself. Still, he was pleased with his ever-increasing strength and endurance. It was something he could take away from this hateful place.

Guys were coming in now and eyeing the weights. Rick left, but not so quickly it would look like they'd flushed him out. After showering, he headed for the library and Mr. B. He was always happy to see Mr. B.

If Rick had known this was his last day, there would have been a few things he would have said to the librarian. But he didn't know. They said hi, Rick mutedly, Mr. B. with the perpetual smile on his round, generous face. Rick sat down with a story called

"Escape from the Maze" that he'd started the day before, nearly the last in a collection called *Amazing Tales from the Ancient Greeks.* He liked to take reading tips from Mr. B. The librarian always seemed to know what he might enjoy. Even his wild hunches, like this one, were on the mark.

Rick hadn't been a reader before. That had come with taking refuge in the library. But he'd discovered that he liked reading, liked it a lot. It enabled him to go places in his head, places very far from Blue Canyon.

He still couldn't sit down and just start reading. It usually took him five or ten minutes. He'd let his mind wander, think about things. As soon as he got bored doing that, he started reading.

Today he was dwelling on Mr. B.'s plant project, how the librarian had kids ordering seeds, sprouting them, growing plants on the library windowsills. Mostly flowering plants. Kids gave them to their parents or guardians, whoever came to visit. Rick noticed that a lot of who came were grandmothers. Like him, quite a few of the kids in Blue Canyon were raised by their grandmothers.

His third-hour science teacher had moved the plant project outside. Kids attacked the bare patch of ground between the flagpole and the Bermuda grass with picks and shovels. Along with the rest, Rick had taken his frustrations out on the ground. The only heads that got busted, despite the misgivings of the administration, were head-sized clods of dirt.

By mid-June a lot of the greens served in the cafeteria were coming out of the garden: lettuce, spinach, parsley, Swiss chard, onions, and radishes. Soon, snow peas and green beans followed, cucumbers and three different kinds of squash.

By early July there was hardly anyone from the science class working in the garden anymore, just Rick and a few others. The desert's midsummer sun was brutal.

But the garden was a safe place for Rick to hang out. The trick was water, drinking gallons of water. He especially liked to see the melons and the pumpkins growing—things that were going to be huge when they finally ripened.

Come late July he was picking the first tomatoes— large, flavorful tomatoes that the cafeteria was serving in thick slices as a side dish. They always went fast. Rick and the few other kids still working in the garden were getting nicknames like the Green Giant, Mr. Tomatohead, Farmerdude, nicknames it was easy to live with. Rick could tell that the fresh food was making his loner status a little more acceptable.

The end, in late August, came with no warning. Overnight the garden had been ripped out back to bare soil. The maintenance men had done it. Too many kids had lost interest, they claimed. There'd never been a garden at Blue Canyon before, and they weren't going to let the maintenance of one get added to their job description.

Rick had expected a big reaction, maybe even a riot. Nothing happened, nothing at all. There was plenty of bad feeling over it, but bad feeling was nothing new. Blue Canyon was a place where kids expressed themselves by mashing moldy oranges into the radiators. The garden had been too good to be true. The real world didn't have gardens and fresh food. The loss of the garden was just one more thing to shrug off.

A month later Rick still hadn't shrugged it off. Mr. B. had advised him to, but he couldn't. There were some things that shouldn't be forgiven and forgotten. Like being led into this place in leg restraints and handcuffs. There were some people who shouldn't be forgiven. Like his parents, like the Honorable Samuel L. Bendix.

Rick realized he'd gone on longer than usual with his reading warm-up. He turned to "Escape from the Maze" and read from the point where the greatest inventor of all time, Daedalus, was fashioning wings for himself and his son, Icarus, so they could fly out of the elaborate puzzle they were imprisoned in.

The wings worked all too well. Once they'd left their island prison behind, Icarus became intoxicated with the sensation of flight and started outflying the birds.

Suddenly Rick recalled that he'd heard this story before. His grandmother had read him a version of it when he was little.

He knew all about the intoxication of flight from way back, from a dream that had come almost nightly. In the dream he always had a miraculous, inexplicable power inside himself: he could actually fly. In the dream all he had to do was spread his arms and he'd begin to levitate higher and higher until he was hovering above the earth. Then he was not only hovering but actually flying above the fields and the treetops and the towns, weightless and peaceful and free.

Dream-flying had been his own great escape—he'd figured that out—a childish fantasy that had been gradually dying over the years and was nearly dead. He couldn't remember having had the flying dream a single time at Blue Canyon.

Rick remembered how Icarus' escape was going to end but he kept reading anyway. Ignoring his father's calls from below, Icarus flew higher and higher until the sun melted the wax holding the invention together, and the boy fell into the sea.

Now Rick realized why he found the story of Icarus so appealing. His own life was a puzzle riddled with dead ends. His own life was a maze.

"From the expression on your face," Mr. B. said from his desk, "you're enjoying that book."

Almost always they talked about what Rick was reading. "Yeah," he said, "I kind of like it."

"So, what do you think of Greek mythology?"

"I can relate to it."

"How so?"

"Things just happen to people for no good reason. Because some god or other gets ticked at them."

"That's the way the ancient Greeks looked at the world, Rick, but we're not ancient Greeks. Americans believe you make your own luck, you know."

Rick didn't really believe it. He was thinking about Killian and wondering about himself. "I suppose."

"Hang in there, Rick. Your break will come. And when it does, you have to be willing to go for it. To see your break for what it is and dare to ride it with all that you've got. Hey, it sure is hot in here, isn't it?"

Because the maintenance men, Rick was tempted to say, have been stealing the brand-new air conditioners so they can resell them. They replace them with reconditioned ones that don't work nearly as well.

He held back. He'd already told his social worker, who'd then gotten fired. He'd made an enormous mistake, especially in telling him he'd seen cash changing hands between a maintenance man and a guard. The guards were being bribed to look the other way, he'd figured out, but corruption in a place like this was no surprise. He'd only ratted on them because he was still so bitter about the garden.

"Yep," Rick said. "It sure is hot." He left the library without saying good-bye to Mr. B.

"See ya soon," they said to each other. But they wouldn't.

3

In the cafeteria line for the evening meal, Killian ghosted up to him and whispered, "Your name is on the cigarettes."

Rick had just reached for a fork and a spoon— there weren't knives—and placed them on his tray. He turned toward the voice. Killian was scuttling away like a crab. Rick looked around quickly, his heart in his throat.

A tray bumped him in the small of his back. "Keep moving, Tomatohead."

He didn't think anyone around him had heard what Killian had whispered. But what did that matter? There were others in this cafeteria, right now, who were eyeing him like hyenas. He would never know who they were.

Your name is on the cigarettes.

Killian wasn't one of them, he knew. Killian was just a fly on the wall.

Your name is on the cigarettes. Everybody knew what that meant. One of the guards was offering two or three kids—seventeen-year-olds, probably—a pack of cigarettes each to beat him to within an inch of his life.

Officially the guards couldn't lay a hand on kids unless it was to restrain them. But when they wanted to hurt somebody it was easily done. Cigarettes were outlawed at Blue Canyon. When kids said, "I'd kill for a cigarette," some of them weren't using a figure of speech.

Rick proceeded mechanically down the cafeteria line, not seeing, not hearing. Floyd, one of the kids working behind the counter, speared a slab of roast beef and made a joke about it being a piece of retread, but Rick didn't hear. He steered toward the table that looked the most open.

When would it come? He hunched over his food, put his hands up to the sides of his head as if he were already warding off the blows.

They wouldn't risk injuring themselves or leaving incriminating marks on their hands. They would use chair legs. All his weight training wouldn't help him, not in a situation like this.

It was only a matter of time until they caught him alone. He'd have to go to the bathroom. He might be sent to the basement to fetch something for someone. There were plenty of ways it could happen, plenty of places.

The guard in that area would take a walk. "Never heard a thing," he'd insist afterward.

Run, he told himself. That's all you can do now. You

can't make it to the end of your sentence. Six weeks is forever. The first beating won't be the last. They'll kill you dead.

Run.

He hadn't eaten a bit. He slipped the fork and the spoon into the pocket of his jeans. Bent at right angles, he'd heard, they made hooks that made it easier to pull yourself over the fence.

Everybody knew how high the fence was. People took its measure every day: sixteen feet, counting three parallel strands of barbed wire on top that leaned in toward the compound.

Kids had escaped while he'd been there, one over the fence and three through the gate. One pretended he was a visitor walking out after lunch. The kid simply waved with supreme confidence and walked on through. Two others, a month apart, rushed the gate while it was open. The gate closed electronically and not very fast.

It was rare, though, for kids ever to get close enough to the gate to rush it. That wasn't going to happen anytime soon. It had to be the fence. People said that you used your jacket to cover the barbed wire, to help you get over the top.

It had to be tonight. The beating would probably come tomorrow.

It was deadly ironic, his name being on the cigarettes. Cigarettes had killed his grandmother. She'd told him when she was dying that it was the cigarettes.

Now it was safest to sit in the TV room, in the very middle of the pack. He was afraid of the edges. Hours went by, and he never got up to go to the bathroom. What programs came on, he couldn't have said.

Through a haze of fear and paranoia, he was trying to think. He was clutching at straws. Some of the kids in his unit had messed with the metal grate over the slot where the air conditioner was missing. Within the last few days they'd loosened the masonry screws from the outside. "Keeping their options open," as they'd put it. Rick himself had never thought about escaping. Now he had to hope that the maintenance men hadn't discovered that the grate was loose and reattached it.

At 9:30 P.M. the TV was killed as usual. Hyperalert, he filed into his unit with the others. At 10:30 Northcut called roll. Then lights out. He got under the sheet with his clothes on, tennis shoes too. It didn't seem as though Northcut had been watching him especially. Did Northcut know that the name of one of his kids was on the cigarettes? Maybe, maybe not.

Rick lay on his back with one hand up to his face as if to ward off a blow. He could hear the second hand on his watch ticking, ticking. Every few minutes he looked at the time. He was wishing that he'd played it all differently. Now was when he needed the protection of a great big kid, an older kid, a mean, crazy guy that nobody would mess with even for cigarettes.

Half an hour after midnight it was deathly quiet at last. Though the night was warm, he slipped on his heavy flannel shirt. He reached under the bed for his red jacket. From under his pillow he took out the fork and the spoon. He bent them carefully at right angles to make grips the width of his hand.

He couldn't stand the tension any longer. *Go!*

Northcut was dozing at his desk as usual. Rick went past the bathroom to the far end of the unit. Gently, he tried the bottom of the grate. It gave.

Tentatively, he pushed it out. The top held but the bottom was free.

Inch by inch, feet first, he climbed out and dropped to the ground. He paused to tie the jacket loosely at his neck.

Looking all around, he crossed the bare patch where the garden used to be, then the threadbare lawn all the way to the fence. With his hooks, he began to pull himself up.

In half a minute he was high on the fence. He dropped the fork and the spoon. Now came the most difficult part, dealing with the wire. With his heart thundering, he hung on with his left hand while he loosened the jacket and placed it as best he could over the barbed wire.

Right leg up, right hand up. He took a deep breath, then made his move, kicking out from the fence and swinging his right leg higher still while clawing with his hands.

Push down, vault the rest of the way up and over.

He felt a sudden pain at his cheekbone as he clawed for a grip in the chain links on the opposite side. He'd snagged his cheek on the wire, but he was over. That was the main thing. He tore his jacket free and lowered himself quickly down the other side. At last he felt the ground under his feet. Now what?

Run.

Run where?

He had no idea.

4

He ran stumbling toward the lights of the interstate. The night was dark, lit only occasionally by the sweep of distant headlights. Behind him the horizon glowed with the greens, yellows, and reds of the neon aurora of Las Vegas.

He reached the on-ramp where a frontage road joined the highway, and he waited. Only three cars in twenty minutes, and they passed him by. Then he heard the chopping of the police helicopter from the direction of Blue Canyon. Northcut had made his middle-of-the-night bed check.

Now Rick could see the helicopter's beam swathing the flats and the arroyos he'd crossed. Just as he was about to bolt for the culvert that ran under the highway, a Nissan Pathfinder with Utah plates stopped for him.

Finally some luck.

The driver seemed very melancholy and possibly drunk. He accepted "up the road" as Rick's destination.

Rick kept his fingers pressed to his wound. It had bled only a little, and he'd blotted it with his red jacket as he ran. The man had seen the wound but hadn't asked about it.

In an hour or so Rick saw the WELCOME TO UTAH sign. The next sign posted the distance to Salt Lake City, 304 miles. He didn't know a thing about Utah, but he had the sudden premonition that he'd better get off the main highway at the next exit.

He walked miles in the dark down the side road. In the middle of the night there was virtually no traffic. Finally a shiny new Dodge Ram pickup with Colorado plates slowed to take a look at him.

The driver was around fifty, with a gray felt cowboy hat and a silver mustache. Rick guessed the man was returning home to Colorado. He was distinguished-looking, like Rick's image of a cattle rancher. The man asked where he was going. Rick's old smile came back to him—"a golden piece of the sun," his grandmother used to call it. "Denver," he answered, because it was the only place in Colorado he could think of. "My mother lives in Denver," he added, because he could see this man expected a story.

"No bag?" the man asked a little suspiciously.

As convincingly as possible Rick replied, "Had it stolen."

"Sorry to hear that," the driver said as he leaned across and opened the passenger door.

The driver shifted quickly through the gears, up to the speed limit. "How'd you get the cut?"

"The guy who stole my bag did it."

"Better get that sewed up. . . . I heard that if you wait past twenty-four hours you'll have a scar for life."

"Well, I have to get to my mother's."

"Does she know you're hitchhiking?"

"She doesn't even know I'm coming. I haven't seen her in a long time."

Whenever he had to invent parent stories, it hurt. Rick turned his head away from the driver, pretended to sleep. Panic rolled over him like a tidal wave. He'd done it now. What would they do to him when they caught him? What would Judge Bendix do? Double his time? What would the guards and the kids do to him when they put him back in Blue Canyon? Why hadn't he been smart enough or brave enough to stay put and take his beating?

At last his weariness overcame his dread, and he drifted into a half sleep. He was vaguely aware of a stop for gas, of the man setting a box of chocolate donuts between them, and the sun coming up. His cheek throbbed all the while. He fell into a deeper sleep and didn't wake for hours. When he woke finally and checked his watch it was one in the afternoon.

"You slept like a mummy," the driver told him.

Rick took a donut. "I felt like one."

The man heard the news coming on and turned the radio up. It was a Las Vegas station, which made Rick nervous. The news was fading in and out; the truck was nearly out of range. At the end of the news it said that a fourteen-year-old male had escaped from the Blue Canyon Youth Detention Center. Rick's name was too garbled to hear, but you could make out some of his description: " . . . brown eyes, dark hair, five foot eight, one hundred and forty-five pounds . . . not

considered dangerous . . . don't take any chances—
notify the police."

The man with the cowboy hat looked over at Rick,
especially at the cut. A little nervously he joked, "That
you?"

"Nope," Rick told him.

For fifty miles or so, Rick thought the driver had
believed him. But then, with his tank still half full, the
man made a gas stop at a tiny desert town called
Hanksville, Utah. Without anything being said, Rick
had the feeling that the ride was over.

The man from Colorado was apologetic. "I don't
know if that's you they're looking for, but I can't take
the chance. You seem like a nice enough kid to me. If
what you told me was true—about having your stuff
stolen—you should call the police. They'll see you get
to your mom's."

Rick went around the side of the station to the
men's room. The knob turned, but the door wouldn't
open, even with a push. As he turned away, he caught
a glimpse of the front end of a Humvee sticking out
from behind the station.

He'd read all about them in magazines, these
overbuilt all-terrain vehicles. They were originally
developed for the military, and they could rumble over
anything in their way. This one, painted in camouflage
grays, yellows, and reds like the colors of the surrounding hills, looked old enough and beat up enough
to be actual military surplus. Now and then he'd seen
newer models on the highway, though he'd never had
the chance to inspect one up close.

As he turned the corner to take a look, there was a
quick movement in the shade under the Humvee. A
dog, suddenly aware of him, lifted its large head and

jowls, bared its teeth, and growled horribly—a rust-colored pit bull. Rick took a step back.

In an instant the dog exploded snarling and barking from under the vehicle and raced at him.

Rick crouched and raised his hands to protect his throat; that's all he was going to be able to do. At the last second the pit bull pulled up short, yet it kept lunging at him while bristling, snapping, growling.

"Jasper!" a voice rasped. "Hold, hold!"

Fingers like claws at the back of Rick's neck dragged him backward. Over his shoulder he saw the grease-stained hand and the angry, angular face of the man in coveralls who ran the gas station. He looked near sixty, with close-cropped gray hair and a chin sharp as a shovel. His face was tinged red by spidery blood vessels just below the surface.

"Git back under the Hummer!" commanded the man with a voice as harsh as a buzz saw.

Curling its lip at Rick, the pit bull slunk back under the vehicle, snarling all the while.

"What are you doing back here?" the man exploded.

"I—I just need the bathroom key."

The gas station man jiggled the knob, then bumped the door open with his shoulder. "Was never locked," he growled.

Nice guy, Rick thought. There was no doubt where the dog had come by its charming personality.

The man from Colorado was standing at the front corner of the building, flashing his credit card at the gas station man. Rick went inside the rest room. Someone had scratched in the mirror, CLEAN YOUR REST ROOM, NUKE.

He guessed that he'd just met Nuke. He was

surprised someone hadn't added a comment about the dog.

The sink was filthy, but at least there was hot water and soap. The cut over his cheekbone looked red-raw, with swelling around the sides. He knew he had to clean it out thoroughly. He splashed warm water on his face, then made a paste in the palm of his hand with the dry soap from the dispenser. On the wound it felt harsh, like gasoline.

Rick stepped outside hoping that his driver had changed his mind, but the Dodge pickup was gone. How was he going to get another ride? There was virtually no traffic here. He looked up and down the road, half expecting to see a patrol car pull into the station with lights flashing.

There was a new vehicle at the pump, a Ford pickup with a camper shell on the back and Arizona plates. The driver, a young, clean-shaven man wearing a Grand Canyon T-shirt, was putting the gas caps back on his dual tanks.

Rick paused at the front corner of the station, waited until the driver went inside to the counter. Neither of the men inside was aware of him. Rick had a desperate idea. There wasn't time to think about it. There was only time to act. Arizona sounded as good as the next place.

He darted to the back of the pickup and tried the camper shell's latch. It turned in his hand. Without hesitating he stepped to the bumper, climbed in the back, and closed the window behind him. The bed of the truck was crammed with coolers, milk crates full of groceries, propane bottles, all sorts of odds and ends.

He worked fast to move forward in the bed of the

pickup. Rearranging milk crates, he managed to wedge himself between two large white coolers. The see-through from the cab into the bed was blocked by equipment. With any luck the driver would return to the truck without looking in the back or through the tinted windows along the sides of the shell.

It worked. For twenty or thirty minutes the pickup sped along the highway. Then it turned onto badly washboarded gravel. Rick kept peeking out the sides, trying to figure out where he was going. The truck was crossing flat mesas, crawling in and out of canyons. Had he just made another mistake? He had a bad feeling this wasn't going to get him anywhere that was going to help him. After several hours the road got so bad that he reached for a twelve-pack of toilet paper to sit on.

Five hours since the gas station, and still he hadn't seen a single indication of civilization. He wondered if he was in Arizona now. He thought of one of the kids in his unit, Manuel Garcia. A month before, Manny had left on a bus for Phoenix, Arizona. His aunt had a cafe there called Penny's Place, and Manny was going to work for her there, live with her family. Rick wondered what Manny and his aunt would say if he showed up at Penny's Place in Phoenix, Arizona. Would they take him in?

Why should they?

Southern California was right next to Arizona. Southern California was where his best foster family had moved to. He'd been close to going with them, being adopted too, and he knew it. He'd even been on their scouting trip to the southern part of the state. "Sure I'd like to," he'd overheard Mrs. Clark telling her husband that day at Disneyland. "Four of our own, and four adopted already. You know I'd like to, but it's a question of the straw breaking the camel's back."

Would they be glad to see him?

Yes, sort of.

Would they keep him?

No.

Would they hide him?

No.

His life was a mountain to climb, and it didn't have handholds.

The pickup stopped. The driver got out of the cab, left the engine running. Rick was afraid the man was about to lift the back of the camper shell.

Instead he heard a click, then ten seconds later a second, identical click. He's locking the hubs, Rick realized, for four-wheel drive.

Half a minute later, with the lights on, the truck started down an incline so steep that everything in the back slid hard toward the front. This was steep, unbelievably steep. The driver was easing the truck down over sudden drops almost like stairs, creeping down the grade in the lowest of his gears.

When the pounding let up for a few seconds, Rick managed to peek out the side. It seemed like the truck was going over the edge of the world. As they passed through a slot in the rim of a cliff, the landscape far below looked like nothing Rick had seen before in his life—a world of fantastically sculpted stone palely lit by the last daylight and strange beyond imagining. It looked like an alien planet.

He wedged himself back into his slot, fought off the crush of a cooler. It took ten minutes for the driver to crawl down the switchbacks to the bottom of the grade. On the flats the driver shifted gears and picked up a little speed. It was getting dark. They were approaching the first of a string of tall buttes, lined up straight as office buildings on a street and silhouetted against the first stars. Where on earth was this?

He was hungry, so hungry. Lifting the lid of the nearest cooler, one of the large white ones, he lurched back in surprise. He was looking into the glazed dead eyes of a baby cow—a half-frozen black-and-white little calf, not gutted or anything. The calf had just been thrown whole into this cooler with some dry ice.

His mind reached for rational explanations but couldn't find any. His heart was hammering out of control like the valves were going to burst. He tried another of the big white coolers. Another dead calf. "Weirdness," he whispered, trying to hold back a cold flash of terror.

The truck stopped. The driver killed the engine and got out.

Rick knew he was going to have to run for it now. His eyes landed on a pack of hot dogs on top of a grocery bag. Grab them, he told himself. You're going to need food. Then he saw that the whole bag was filled with hot dogs. What would anyone want with this many hot dogs?

He took just one pack. Through the window now he could see two men talking, the driver and a slim man with a full beard.

Rick eased the rear window of the camper shell up, slid over the tailgate, crouched, and peeked at the silhouettes of the two men. They were standing in front of three canvas wall tents erected in a row on wood platforms. A large tarp had been pitched across from the tents over an area Rick couldn't see. He saw a white fiberglass kennel cage, but he didn't see a dog. He'd had enough of dogs for one day. A second Ford pickup with a camper shell was parked next to a large fuel drum on a metal stand. This was quite an encampment.

The two men, Rick realized, must be about to unload the groceries and the dead calves. He had to make his move now.

Keeping the truck between him and them, Rick stepped softly into the darkness on the pavementlike natural surface of sandstone. A gigantic rock formation nearby, like a petrified ship in a petrified sea, promised cover.

5

Rick had hoped the rocks would give off heat during the night and keep him warm, but they didn't. He shivered for hours under a clear black sky blazing with stars. The moon rose after midnight and threw cold light on the cliffs towering above the camp. Finally he slept. His dreams took him on a jangled and confusing ride until he found himself in the comfort of his old familiar flying dream.

When he was younger, he'd been able to keep the dream going all night—hovering, weightlessly hovering, with his arms outspread. It had started when he was growing up on the Mendocino coast, in California. The first time he'd had the dream, he'd flown above the lighthouse where his grandmother had worked when he was little, before she got the job managing the trailer park at Fort Bragg.

That first dream was still vivid in his memory. His grandmother had stepped outside the lighthouse gift shop. He could see her down there, looking all around for him. Finally she looked *up*. She saw him flying above the lighthouse. She beckoned him to come down.

In the flying dream people were always beckoning him to come down.

Tonight he was hovering above the yard at Blue Canyon. It was Northcut, the guard, who came out of a building and tried to wave him down. Rick hovered a little higher. Some teachers came out and called for him to come down, Mr. B. even. With a shake of his head he floated even higher until he could see the entire square shape of the compound defined by the fence. Now all the kids were flooding into the yard. The entire yard was filled with faces, too far below to identify. He could still see their arms, though, motioning for him to come back.

It made him feel both happy and sad to be out of reach, out of everybody's reach.

The high desert cold in the hour before dawn woke Rick up. Instantly he was aware of the throbbing at his cheekbone. Then he recalled his dream. He could still see the compound at Blue Canyon from the air and people beckoning. The old image of flying above the lighthouse came to mind, and he remembered the ancient-looking sign he used to puzzle over at the entrance to the museum gift shop. The sign said PRAY FOR THOSE WHO ARE LOST. He wouldn't have puzzled over it now. It was about people like him.

He missed his grandmother, more than he'd allowed himself to miss her in a long time. He could remember her voice, her eyes. She hadn't been that old when she died, only forty-seven. Her hair wasn't even gray.

"Life isn't fair," he'd pointed out to her once, on the subject of his mother.

"Tough beans, kid," his grandmother replied. "How can *life* be fair? Only people can be fair."

It was close to dawn, but a few stars were still out. The horizon was glowing with pinks and oranges and lavenders. Rick stood up, shivered, and shook. At the sound of a motor starting he skittered up a mound of smooth sandstone to peer over the top. The supply truck was pulling out, going back the same way it had come in.

For a second Rick wondered if he should run after it and try to holler it down. Maybe he could come up with some kind of story.

Too late anyway, he realized. The driver was making good time on the flats. In a few minutes the truck would be climbing the steep grade up the switchbacks.

He remembered the dead calves. It was better not to have anything to do with these people.

He needed to get out of here. He shivered again. It wasn't just the cold.

The more frightened he became, the more he was drawn to a desperate solution. He needed the truck he was looking at, the one that remained in camp. Not to go back the way he'd come, up that horrible road, but to head east. The road in the direction of the approaching sunrise looked much easier.

He wouldn't be stealing the truck. He would leave it at the first major road he came to, and he'd leave a note. What other choice did he have? Wait for a vehicle to come by, hope to hitch a ride out here on the far side of the moon?

He could hope that the bearded man had left the keys in the ignition. In this world populated by rocks instead of human beings, that seemed possible.

Hurry, before the sun rises.

He crept to the truck and peered inside. The keys were there, just as he'd pictured them.

A minute later he was behind the wheel and raising a cloud of dust. The gears ground horribly as he tried to shift into third. A light in the panel said he was in four-wheel drive. He'd leave it that way; he knew nothing about operating the stubby secondary gearshift. In his rearview mirror he saw the bearded man burst out of the tent. The man didn't even try to run after him, just stood there with his hands on his hips and gaped in disbelief.

Rick drove fast through sandy gullies and across terraces of solid rock sprinkled with narrow-leafed yucca and prickly pear cactus and the only trees able to survive there, scrubby pinyon pines and junipers. He stuffed hot dogs one after the other into his mouth, the three he hadn't eaten the night before. The deteriorating road headed down the spine of the ridge past sand dunes that spilled onto a long, parched clearing dotted with bunchgrass.

Rick saw no vehicles, no people, but he assumed that if he kept driving he would eventually put this bizarre and threatening landscape behind him. Five miles from where he'd started, however, the road abruptly dead-ended at a cluster of slender, standing formations that looked like dozens of hundred-foot giants balancing bowling pins on their heads. One of them even appeared to have an eye. It looked like a cyclops from Greek mythology.

He knew he hadn't passed a fork. This really was

the end of the road. Could he go on foot from here?

A five-minute run down the trail that led from road's end brought him to the edge of an abyss.

Rick was looking almost straight down, a thousand feet or more, at a great river winding its way through a monumental corridor of stone. He stepped back, light-headed, disbelieving. What was this place? Where in the world was he?

Looking into the sun across the river, Rick could see another world of weirdly sculpted badlands with a mountain range beyond. To the north stretched more canyons and towering mesas, another mountain range. As far as he could see there wasn't a single building, a single road. He'd reached the dead end of nowhere.

There was only one direction to go: back the way he'd come. He was going to have to make a run for it past the bearded man's camp, up the grade onto the plateau, and back to Hanksville.

He turned the truck around and drove toward the standing red buttes and the tall red cliffs beyond. The rear end scraped badly as he forced his way too fast through a gully. After that he was able to pick up some speed.

In the rearview mirror he saw the plume of red dust he was raising. He was going fast, so fast he hit his head on the cab roof and bit his tongue. Now he was putting the string of buttes behind him and approaching the camp. He held his breath.

No one was there. Had the bearded man called ahead, called the police? Probably he had a radio or a cell phone.

For the first time Rick noticed the two-way radio mounted by the base of the gearshift. A coiled cord led to a push-to-talk mike among the clutter on the bench seat of the truck. If he was lucky, this radio was the man's only communication link to the outside.

He put the camp behind him and raced in and out of the gullies toward the base of the boulder-strewn slopes ahead. It was here that the road, if it could be called a road, took advantage of a natural interruption in the seemingly endless march of vertical cliffs under the rim of the plateau. He knew it would be slow going when the road got bad, which it would as soon as it started to climb. There were so many places to hide, the bearded man could appear at any second. Rick held his breath.

He was climbing the first hairpin, already a couple of hundred feet above the rocky plain. As he came around the turn, he found the narrow passage barricaded with rocks and small boulders. The man from the camp, with a full red-brown beard beginning to gray, his faded denim shirt unbuttoned, was sitting on his roadblock with his hands on his hips and breathing heavily from exertion.

A few feet closer and Rick noticed an angry-looking scar on the man's cheekbone, unnaturally smooth and white in comparison to the rest of his face, which was deeply tanned, lined, and leathery.

There was no mistaking the magnitude of the man's anger.

For a moment Rick thought of trying to race the truck backward. But he knew he'd only drive it off the road and roll it over.

Now this. Another dead end. His life was nothing but an endless succession of dead ends.

6

He looked away from the furious blue eyes and the hard white scar.

"What do you think you're doing?" the bearded man yelled as he yanked open the door of the pickup. "Get out of my truck!"

Rick jumped out, backed away slowly. "I wasn't going to—I didn't mean to . . ."

"Who are you anyway, and how did you get here?"

Rick kept backing up, trying to think what he should say. The truth? A lie? The guy was so mad, he was afraid to say anything.

"Get back in the truck," the man ordered.

Rick went around to the passenger side and got in. He was relieved that the man hadn't taken his fists to him or pulled out a gun.

The bearded man set to work with a vengeance,

tossing rocks off the road, then jumped into the driver's seat, slammed the door, and started backing down the grade.

All Rick could think about was Blue Canyon. They would put him back in Blue Canyon for sure. His life was over.

The man drove to his camp without once glancing at Rick. In camp the man continued to ignore him as he brewed a pot of coffee. He must be trying to figure out what to do with me, Rick thought.

The man with the scar poured himself a cup of coffee and sat down on a lawn chair. "So what are you doing here?" he asked suddenly. "Where's your stuff? You must have a backpack or a sleeping bag somewhere."

"I don't have any stuff," Rick answered. "It all got stolen . . . out on the highway."

"Then how did you get here? My supply truck? Did you hide in the back? Is that it?"

"Yeah, that's it. Look, I really wasn't going to steal your truck. I was going to leave it as soon as I got back to the highway."

"You could get *hurt* pulling a stunt like that."

"I already got hurt," Rick said, motioning toward his cheekbone. "I gotta get something on this. I'm worried about it."

The man pointed toward the tent on the end, directly across from his kitchen. "I got a first-aid kit in there—look for a white ammo can with a red cross on it."

The tent turned out to be the man's commissary. Its shelves were stocked with canned goods. There was even a refrigerator and a chest freezer, each hooked up to a propane bottle. Rick found the first-aid kit and started digging through it. He pulled out a bottle of peroxide, some antibiotic cream, a mirror, and a box of bandages.

Rick cleaned up his wound in the man's open-air kitchen where he could make use of the big water jug. He smeared on some cream, then closed the cut tight with two butterfly bandages. It wasn't as good as stitches—he'd still get a scar—but it was the best he could do.

The man came over to take a look. "Not bad," he said. "You'll live."

Rick was relieved that the man was lightening up. Maybe this was a chance to try to be friendly. "So, what part of Arizona is this?"

"Arizona?" There was surprise and a bit of mockery in the man's deep, reverberating baritone. "You're in Utah, kid. Canyonlands National Park. You're at the edge of the Maze and about ten miles west of where the Green River joins the Colorado. You probably saw the Colorado down at the end of your little ride."

"Maze?" Rick asked. "Like 'rats in a maze'?"

"That's right," the man said with a wry twist of humor creeping across his face, "and you're the rat."

Rick laughed. "So where's this Maze you're talking about? Can I see it from here?"

"We're about a half mile away from where it starts. It's a whole network of canyons sitting below this bench my camp is on. The Maze is a thirty-square-mile puzzle in sandstone. You're at the end of the line, my dubious friend, about as remote as you can get in the lower forty-eight."

"Did you say this is a national park? No way. I've been to Yosemite, in California. People were elbow to elbow."

"This park's different, one of a kind. And this is the most rugged district in it. Most of the visitors are north and east of here, across the rivers. This part's really hard to get to."

"Tell me about it."

The man seemed about to laugh but stopped himself. It was a hopeful sign. Maybe this was going to turn out okay after all, Rick thought. It might even be a good thing—at least for the time being—that he'd ended up in such a desolate place. Whatever the calves in the coolers were all about, this guy didn't feel dangerous. Eccentric and prickly, but not dangerous.

"So does this place get patrolled by a park ranger?"

"Not as much as it used to. The ranger station— back on the flats about halfway to Hanksville— burned to the ground last spring. There's no ranger there right now."

"How soon will you be driving out with your truck, like to go to town?"

"Thinking about leaving, are you? It'll be two or three months before I'll be driving out for anything. I've got no reason to go to town."

"Two or three *months*?" Rick realized he sounded panicky. "Will that other guy come back soon? The guy I came in with?"

"That was Josh. He comes in every two weeks. Should be back the evening of October the fifteenth."

"Doesn't anybody else come in here?"

"Hikers, occasionally. You know, you could walk out to Hanksville if you really wanted to. It's sixty some miles, but at least it's October."

"What do you mean?"

"I mean, the heat's finally let up. You wouldn't die

of heatstroke, like you would in the summer. Daytime temperatures are downright pleasant this time of year. It hasn't been getting any warmer than the seventies. It's high here, you know—this is over five thousand feet in elevation."

Rick was trying to imagine walking sixty some miles over this kind of terrain. No doubt this man could. The face that showed above the graying beard had been burned to leather and hardened by the elements and was furrowed with canyons of its own.

"So, you want to tell me how you got that cut?" the man pressed.

"Yeah, I guess you're wondering how all this happened, what I'm doing here and all. I guess I owe you an explanation—"

"On second thought"—the man with the scar interrupted—"save your energy. I'm sorry I asked." His deep blue eyes had a weary, ancient quality Rick hadn't noticed before. "You don't have to make up a story for me. You weren't going to tell me the truth anyway, were you? Let's just start with some introductions. I'm Lon Peregrino. What's your name?"

"Rick," he said truthfully. "My name's Rick Walker."

7

"I've got work to do. You saw where the food is. Help yourself if you're hungry."

With that, the man with the scar went back to his routines as if Rick weren't there. He set up a large tripod-mounted spotting scope near his kitchen, got a big pair of binoculars from his tent, sat down, and started watching something up on the cliffs high above.

Rick walked over toward the commissary tent, then stopped and squinted toward the rugged surfaces of the cliffs high above. What could the man be looking at? Rick saw pinnacles, spires, coves, boulders perched on slanting ledges, but he couldn't tell what the man had his scope trained on. What did this guy do out here in the middle of nowhere? What were the dead calves all about?

Rick pulled a lawn chair aside, where he'd be out of the way, and ate a bowl of cereal, then a second and a third. He watched the bearded man disappear into his tent and return a minute later with a small black electronic instrument clipped to his belt—a two-way radio identical to the one in the truck. As he walked across the pavementlike stone surface in front of the tents, he jacked an attachment into the radio. Once its cross members were unfolded, it proved to be a small handheld antenna.

Lon Peregrino flicked the power on and aimed the antenna at the cliffs. He pointed it slowly back and forth, picking up a pattern of beeps. Just then Rick's eye caught the movement of a very large dark bird flying across the rim. It landed on a pinnacle jutting out from the cliffs. An eagle?

Suddenly Lon packed up his radio and his scope, jumped in his truck, and drove out of camp without a word.

Strange guy, Rick thought, and moody as the wind.

A few minutes later Rick spotted the truck crawling up the switchbacks toward the top of the cliffs. He decided to have a look around camp while he was alone and had the chance.

Three trails led out of camp across patches of red dirt and wound their way among the scrubby trees and the boulders that had fallen from the cliffs. One trail led to a plastic shower bag suspended from a juniper limb. He felt the bag. The water was warm, almost hot.

The second trail led to a portable toilet behind a boulder as big as a small house.

The third led to a spring at the base of the rubble-strewn slope that flared from the towering cliffs. A metal pipe had been jammed between the rock layers where the seepage was strongest. A strong flow of water ran out of the pipe onto the ground and made a miniature oasis wherever it touched. The view from the spring opened onto endless stony distances and sky that was hard and turquoise blue, solid as a gemstone. It was eerie how empty it all was.

Walking back toward camp, Rick was following what looked like a game trail among the junipers and pinyon pines. It led toward a small clearing. He brushed a limb aside and pushed on through. No more than two arm's lengths away and to the side, some large living thing suddenly hissed at him. He recoiled, instinctively shielding his face with his forearms.

It was an eagle, an immense white-headed, white-tailed bald eagle! He backed out the way he'd come, his heart thundering. Through the branches of a stubby tree he could see the huge bird, still in the same place, fidgeting along a smooth pole that had apparently been lashed between trees across a corner of the clearing. Why had it let him get so close? Why hadn't it flown?

Creeping a little closer, he found the answer. Leather thongs restrained the bird's feet.

What was Lon Peregrino doing with a captive eagle?

A minute later Rick came across a yellow mountain bike behind the tents. It was a Diamondback, the same brand he'd admired in the ads in the bike magazines in Mr. B.'s library. There were also two long plastic tubes around twenty feet long, with screw-in lids. He wondered what was inside but didn't attempt to open them.

On a bicycle, Rick thought, he could make it back to Hanksville easily. Lon hadn't told him about the bike. Should he take it right now?

Maybe he should wait a few days until the search for him had died down. Then go.

Go where?

The coast of California. Fort Bragg.

And do what? Hide out in a sea cave? His grand-mother was gone.

Dead ends every direction he turned.

He was still hungry. He went back to look for some-thing more to eat, found a banana. He sat on a lawn chair in the sun. Time had slowed almost to a stand-still.

If he was thinking about staying here any longer, he needed to know more about Lon Peregrino and what this encampment was all about. He found him-self standing in front of Lon's tent. The door flaps were untied. He took a step up onto the wood floor of the tent.

The first things he noticed were two helmets on the floor under the man's cot, stowed neatly in front of a large duffel bag. Motorcycle helmets, apparently. He could picture the man with the scar as a Harley rider. . . .

Across from the cot were a footlocker and a small dresser with a manual typewriter on top of it and the fold-up radio antenna. Next to the head of his cot was a crate for a nightstand. In addition to candles it had a half dozen fossil shells on it and a book called *Walden*.

Holding his breath, Rick opened the top drawer of Lon's dresser. He was looking at Lon's radio, the one he'd had clipped to his belt, a couple of baseball caps, a red bandanna, a couple pairs of sunglasses, a long bone-handled sheath knife, and a thin wallet.

With a quick glance over his shoulder, Rick opened the wallet. A hundred-dollar bill, a twenty, a few ones. No credit cards, no photos, no receipts, no odds and ends. Lon Peregrino's driver's license was from Arizona. His address was listed as Cliff Dweller's Lodge, Vermilion Cliffs, Arizona.

Rick put the wallet back and reached for an item he'd overlooked—one of those open-up photo holders, the kind for displaying one large photo inside. Did the man have a family somewhere?

Inside was a yellowed clipping from a newspaper in McCall, Idaho. It was a photograph of a boy about Rick's age with a bald eagle on his arm. The boy was Lon Peregrino, Rick realized. There was the scar, only darker, fresher. The eyes were the same, the mouth was the same. Rick sat down on the cot and began to read the caption under the photo. He'd gotten no further than "Kenny McDermott proudly displays eagle" when he heard the sound of an approaching vehicle.

He's lying about his name, Rick realized, as he hastily closed the folder and returned it as best he could to its former position. He's using an alias. Why would he do that?

With a peek out the door, he dashed across the clearing, expecting to see Lon's truck. To his surprise it wasn't Lon. Rick panicked as he realized that he recognized this vehicle. It was the Humvee from the gas station in Hanksville, parking several hundred feet away where the spur into the camp left the road. Rick's view was blocked by junipers and boulders, but he heard two doors slam, then that buzz saw voice he'd heard before. "Wind your window up. Leave it open enough so he's got plenty of ventilation."

The pit bull. Thank goodness they're leaving it in the Humvee.

The men were walking right toward camp. Friends of Lon's? Soundlessly, Rick backed out through the kitchen and took cover behind a cluster of boulders. He would have run farther, but there wasn't enough cover. They were too close.

Now Rick could see them, two men in jeans, western shirts, and cowboy hats. The gray-haired older man under the brown felt Stetson, with chin sharp as a shovel, was the pit bull owner from the gas station in Hanksville. He was weathered and hard as an old fencepost, and he carried himself erect and alert like a soldier.

The second one, under a straw cowboy hat, was a bigger man and somewhat younger, maybe in his forties. A barrel of a man on thin legs, he wore cowboy boots and had a large silver buckle that was mostly obscured by his belly. There was attitude—possibly a sneer—on his fleshy face as he looked around the camp. He was wearing a pair of binoculars around his neck, and he was jiggling an empty five-gallon water jug with one finger. As they halted opposite the first tent, he set the jug down and lifted the binoculars to his eyes. For a long time he scanned the cliffs above. "Neither hide nor hair," he finally reported.

"Good," rasped the pit bull's owner. "He's still behind the blind watching his birds. He'd have to come practically to the edge of the cliff to see down here. If he does, he'll be real obvious."

The one with the binoculars trained on the cliffs said contemptuously, "Can you imagine getting paid to watch vultures?" His voice had none of the gravel or authority of the older man's. It sounded peevish and small.

"Complete idiocy, but what can you expect from the government? Keep watching the rim, Gunderson. I'm gonna take a couple of minutes to look around before we go for water."

"We don't really need water, Nuke."

"I know that," came the testy reply. "But if we don't at least look like we're getting water, we don't have any reason for being in his camp."

Rick's skin was crawling. These men were definitely not friends of Lon's. What were they doing here?

"Okay, okay," Gunderson said. "We'll act like we're here to get water. What I'd really like to do is blow this guy's camp to kingdom come. What a pain. I still say we should just shoot those birds—or poison 'em. No way they'd put another batch in here once these were all killed. They'd pull the camp and do it somewhere else."

"Real smart, Gunderson. That would be in every newspaper in the country. This is a big deal to the government, these endangered birds. This whole area would be swarming with law enforcement—mostly federal."

"So we have to pull our stuff out of here?"

"You don't seem to get the picture. This is a much bigger problem than we originally thought. We've never had this situation before—somebody right down here at the Maze, twenty-four hours a day, right in our old camp. I talked to this guy last week. He or somebody like him could be here for the next twenty years! This project just goes on and on. Typical government work."

"Can't we just wait, Nuke? Are you sure we have

to pull all our stuff out? Can't we just see how it goes with this guy?"

"You'll have plenty of time to wait if we get caught—wait for your jail sentence to run out. Keep watching the rim with those field glasses. I'm going to have a look in those tents."

"How come?"

"It's called intelligence. Find out what he's got and what he doesn't got."

"He doesn't got a brain, that's what I think. You'd have to be a total fool to baby-sit vultures . . . to live like this."

Vultures? Rick wondered. Endangered vultures?

When Nuke returned from Lon's tent, Gunderson asked, "What's he got?"

"Secondhand junk. Books, clothes, another radio. No camera, unless he's got one in the truck."

"That's good. At least he doesn't have a camera. He got any weapons? Ammunition? Bet he don't."

"Sheath knife was all I could see. He could have a gun in his truck, but I doubt it. You know the type, probably hates guns. Let's go over to the spring, just in case he's watching, and then get out of here. We have some work to do."

Rick kept hidden until the two men returned from the spring and cleared out. The Humvee drove down the road to the east, in the direction of the buttes. What was it they had to take out of here? What were they up to that could land them in prison?

8

The camp was in shadow and Lon still hadn't returned. Rick couldn't get the image of those two "visitors" out of his head. They reminded him of the guards back at Blue Canyon. He wished Lon would come back.

Who was this bird expert really? Rick wished he knew if the man could be trusted. Why had he changed his name? Had he committed a crime? Abandoned a family?

Rick realized he should be hiding some food, at least enough to keep him from starving if he had to run for it. He went into the commissary tent. A couple of cans of tuna, a couple of chunk chicken, and one of the small canned hams wouldn't be missed. But where could he stash them? The Maze was supposed to be nearby. The Maze sounded like a perfect place to hide out if it came to that.

He threw his supplies in a sack and walked out onto the rolling sea of smooth white rock that undulated from the edge of the camp. Ten minutes later he found himself reeling back from the very edge of a stupendous drop into thin air.

Rick caught his breath and calmed his heart. This had to be the Maze. Cautiously he crept close to the edge of the cliff. He was looking down two or more hundred feet into a very narrow canyon banded spectacularly with horizontal layers of rock. The cliff walls looked like a cross section of a ten-layer cake. Underneath the thick white frosting at the top came alternating layers of pink, buff, and raspberry. The thick swath of red halfway down was the most eye-catching of all.

Rick could barely believe this place was real, even though he was staring right at it.

He looked to see if he could spot a route down into the canyon but couldn't see one. Within a couple hundred yards the canyon deepened to four hundred feet or more. As it disappeared around the bend, the canyon was still so narrow that its depth exceeded its width.

Lifting his eyes to the rim, Rick saw the rims of more and more canyons beyond this one, all glowing with the flat golden light of evening. He was at the edge of a vast natural puzzle of intricate canyons cut deep in a petrified sea. The Maze.

Rick picked a spot to hide the canned goods under the roots of a stunted juniper, then sat down and tried to figure out what to do next. He thought about how ironic it was that he'd landed in this place. A maze was nothing new to him. He'd been trapped in one for a long, long time.

A reflected flash of light from high above on the red cliffs caught his eye: a mirror on the bird expert's truck. The Ford was inching its way down the switchbacks. Rick had no real sense of where he stood with the mysterious "Lon Peregrino," but he knew he needed cover. His safest option had to be staying right here, in the middle of nowhere, at least for a while.

But was it too late? Had the man already reported him? From up above, on the plateau? Rick had to know.

Lon got out of the truck and started getting himself some supper. He looked preoccupied and acted like Rick wasn't even there. Rick felt he'd been tuned out, as if someone had hit the mute button on the TV, as if he'd been switched off for Lon's convenience.

Cuisine for tonight, at least for Peregrino, was cold hot dogs. No buns, no mustard or relish, just hot dogs. And a green salad. Lon arranged the hot dogs and the salad on a plastic plate, then sat down on a folding chair in front of his kitchen tarp. Rick cautiously pulled up a chair next to the bearded enigma.

"So, what were you looking at up there? Birds?"

Lon seemed genuinely startled to see him. "Oh, jeez," he said. "I'll bet you're hungry. Want a hot dog?"

"Thanks. Mind if I try cooking it? Heat it up in some water?"

"Suit yourself. Like I said, help yourself to whatever you want. I'm not much of a cook."

Rick heated up some hot dogs, wrapped them in slices of bread, found some mustard and relish. He took his plate back over by Lon and sat down on the lawn chair, ready for another try at conversation. He didn't want to start right out telling him about the men. He had to plan this, do it right.

"What kind of birds are you studying? That is what you're doing out here, isn't it—studying birds?" Rick thought that sounded like a safe beginning.

"Actually," Lon answered, "I'm doing more than studying them. This is a release project. We're reintroducing six birds to the wild. They're *condors,* North American condors. Largest bird on the continent— nine-and-a-half-foot wingspan—also the most endangered. Ever heard of 'em?"

Rick tried to remember if he ever had. He shook his head.

"Ice Age survivor, nature's most magnificent flying machine."

There was a tone in the man's voice of deep respect, almost of awe. Keep him talking, Rick told himself. This is going well. "'Ice Age survivor'?" he asked. "I don't understand what you mean."

"I mean just that. They're survivors from the time of the Ice Ages. The last Ice Age ended about ten thousand years ago."

"To tell you the truth, I never understood what that was all about."

The man studied him closely to see if he was putting him on.

Rick wasn't faking it, or at least not very much. He was intrigued by the idea of rare vultures.

"This spot where we're sitting wasn't covered by glaciers," the man who called himself Lon continued, "but a lot of North America was. The Southwest was cooler and wetter back then. More grass, more flowers, big trees where they can't grow now—the climate supported a lot of big-time animals."

"Like woolly mammoths," Rick guessed. "And saber-toothed tigers." He was remembering the visit he'd made with the Clarks to the famous tar pits in L.A.

"Bull's-eye," the biologist said approvingly. His deep baritone voice sounded friendly. Was the man willing to be friendly? Should he tell him now about the two men?

Lon disappeared into the commissary tent and returned with a box of cake donuts. He took one and handed the box over to Rick. "Picture giant animals moving right through here, the hunted and the hunters. Giant bison, giant ground sloths, camels, mastodons, a bear bigger than the grizzly, the dire wolf. Lots of kills, lots of carrion to get cleaned up afterward by scavengers."

Rick was making connections. "Must have been some *mega*vultures back then, like mega everything else."

"That's right. There *was* a megavulture, as you call it. Not all the meat eaters depended on tooth and claw. The great virtue of this one was patience. This bird was capable of soaring for a hundred, two hundred miles with hardly a beat of its wings while scanning the ground for a dinner table that was already set. All those other giant animals I mentioned are extinct. The condor was the most adaptable. It has at least a million years behind it, and it's still around, but barely."

Suddenly one of the condors flew above the rim, and Rick pointed. He was thrilled that he'd spotted it. The biologist hadn't noticed.

Lon reached for his binoculars hanging from the spotting scope. "He's up a good three hundred feet. Best flight yet! Must be M4!"

After a few seconds Lon passed the binoculars. Rick located the bird. With huge wide wings held flat and a large, ruddering tail, the "megavulture" was holding its position against the wind. At the tips of its wings, individual feathers curving slightly upward extended a long way, like fingers.

"That's a condor you're looking at," the man said reverently. "They're still around. Very few, but you're looking at one. Their chances for survival are considered extremely remote."

"If it's a vulture, how come the skin isn't red?"

"Because they're only six months old. At five years or so, at maturity, all that gray skin on its neck and head will turn orange or yellow or a combination of the two. The adults also develop large, spectacular white patterns on the underside of their wings."

Rick watched the huge bird come in for a landing up on the rim, on a pinnacle in front of the cliffs. "Six months old? Did I hear you right?"

"They're just learning to fly. They were hatched in zoos out in California."

"How come you didn't release their parents with them, to teach 'em stuff?"

"We need the older birds for breeding, to get the population up. There aren't any more mature condors left in the wild, none. They were down to *nine* individuals when the scientists decided to capture them and try to save the species by captive breeding. The adults we have now would just fly off and starve to death. They were hatched in zoos too—don't know the first thing about locating food and a hundred other things about being a condor. These fledglings will figure it out gradually as they're learning to fly, and they won't fly too far away at first."

"M4—the one we were looking at—is he something special?"

"Oh, yeah, he's special. The day we released them—just ten days ago—he flew all the way out to that pinnacle he's on right now. That was quite a feat for a condor fledgling. I mean, flying off the edge of a cliff with nothing but eight hundred feet of air under your wings, when you've only flown short bursts in a pen . . . that takes guts even for a juvenile, who's naturally long on stupidity."

Was there a trace of mockery in the man's voice? If so, it was a good joke. And Lon was smiling.

Rick decided to seize the moment, take a chance. "You have radio contact with the outside world?" he ventured.

"Sure," Lon replied, without sounding cagey. He pointed to a high distant plateau with a prow like a ship. "There's a repeater over there on the Island in the Sky."

Spill it, Rick told himself. Just ask him. But he hesitated, not wanting to make a mistake.

The biologist eyed him critically. "What is it you're getting at?"

"Okay . . . did you radio me in? Like to the sheriff or something? Is somebody coming in here tomorrow to pick me up?"

This time it was the man who hesitated, studying him as he squirmed. "Not unless you want somebody to."

Rick was confused. "I don't, believe me."

Silence settled in again. Rick couldn't read this man at all. "How come you didn't turn me in?"

The bird biologist stroked his beard thoughtfully where it was graying, over his chin. "A guy named Ernie," he said whimsically.

"Who's he?"

Lon waved dismissively. "Doesn't matter . . . a man

I used to know. Let's say it was on a hunch, for personal reasons."

Once again, silence ebbed into the gulf between them.

"You're obviously between a rock and a hard place," the man continued finally.

"You can say that again," Rick admitted.

"Let me just ask this. Have you hurt anybody? Is that what you're running from?"

"It's not that," Rick answered quietly. "No, I didn't hurt anybody."

"Somebody hurt *you*? Put that cut on your face? Father, stepfather?"

Rick shook his head. "I don't have one. Used to have a foster father—more than one. One of 'em taught me to drive. . . ." With a grimace he added, "As much as I know, that is."

The man turned his intense blue eyes on him. Rick thought he might be seeing a willingness to understand, but how could he know for sure that this man with the double identity would be fair?

"If I tell you where I came from, you'll have to report me."

The man with the scar thought about it. He thought about it a long time. "Can't answer that. Keep your secret if you need to."

"I want to stay here. I *need* to."

Lon was about to say something, but Rick cut him off. "There were two guys in your camp this afternoon. I think you might be in danger."

"What do you mean?" Lon asked quickly.

"There were two men in your camp while you were up on the cliff. They were driving an old beat-up Humvee."

"I heard a vehicle from up above but didn't get a

look. Must have been Nuke Carlile, from the gas station in Hanksville. He comes to get water from the spring."

"He got water, but he didn't need water."

At that, one of Lon's eyebrows rose. "What do you mean?"

"I heard them talking. They didn't know I was here. I heard a lot of things."

Lon was interested, definitely interested. "What kind of things?"

"About you and your birds. Your visitors weren't big fans."

Peregrino's eyes blazed. "If you have something to tell me, kid, spit it out. What did you hear?"

Rick told it all, slowly, carefully. The man listened intently, worrying his beard all the while. Afterward Lon grilled him on the particulars, especially about the possibility of the birds being shot or poisoned.

"The guy named Gunderson was just a hothead. Liked to talk big."

"Like blowing my camp to kingdom come? Not a pretty picture."

Rick nodded. "But Carlile was the guy in charge, no question. He said they weren't going to mess with the birds, because it would bring law enforcement, like I told you. They were afraid of going to jail and all. He said they were going to pull out their stuff, whatever that meant, because you were too close and were going to stay a long time."

The biologist looked away to the stony distances, his forehead furrowed and his blue eyes hard. "They must be pothunters," he said finally.

"Pothunters? What's that?"

"Looters. They pillage ancient Native American sites on public land. In this area they're mostly after seed jars and water jars and so on—thousand-year-old pottery. Unfortunately there's a strong black market, and that stuff's really valuable. This whole area is rich with Fremont and Anasazi sites. Nobody knows the Maze area better than Carlile, according to the man himself—he told me so."

"You've met him, I take it?"

"Just a week ago, down here, shortly after we released the birds. He informed me I'd taken 'his' campsite. Said he'd developed the spring behind camp a long time ago. I told him about my permit, told him anyone and everyone was welcome to come for water at any time—it's all public land. He took exception to that term. He said, 'You mean, *government* land.'"

"I didn't mention that he made some kind of crack about you working for the government."

"Shows what they know. I work for the Condor Project, which is supported by private donations from individuals all over the country, foundations, corporations. . . . Yeah, the federal government kicks in too. The U.S. Fish and Wildlife Service selected us to do the work. Is there anything else they might've said? Carlile talked about cameras. Anything else to indicate what he was looking for?"

"That was it," Rick said, but in the moment he said it there was a twinge of doubt. There might have been another detail, but if so, it had slipped his mind.

Suddenly the biologist stood up. "I'm gonna make a call," he said, "and then I'm gonna hit the rack. Look, you can stay here a few days. We'll see how it goes and we'll take it from there. Sleep in the middle tent. There's a sleeping bag and a pillow, candles on the nightstand. Help yourself to anything in the bookcase if you feel like it. Thanks for telling me all this."

"Were they right about you not having a gun?"

"Yeah, they were right. Say, one thing I have to warn you about, Rick, if you're going to be around: I live out like this for a reason. I work alone by preference whenever I get the chance. I do a lot better with birds than I do with people. Sometimes I'm not that easy to be around—I work on my head a lot. So don't expect too much."

With that the biologist went to his truck, got in, and shut the door behind him. He raised the mike to his mouth. Rick wasn't going to be able to hear a thing he said.

Was Lon going to say where he got his information?

Somehow he didn't think so.

Lon had promised at least a couple of days. He had a few days to hide and rest, heal up the hammering cut in his face. Lon might let him pack some food and water, maybe even let him use the bicycle to get back to the highway.

Then what?

9

The next morning the biologist wandered off by himself to sip his coffee. Rick wanted to ask about the eagle, the one he'd discovered tethered behind the camp, but wasn't sure how to bring it up. He waited until Lon made his way back toward the kitchen, settled into his favorite lawn chair, and started adjusting his spotting scope.

"Are you studying eagles too?" Rick asked.

"Nope, just condors," Lon grunted.

Try again, Rick told himself. "I saw that big eagle tied to the branch behind camp. Are you going to release it?"

"Oh, so you discovered Sky. I wish I could release her, but she's missing most of her left wing," Lon replied grimly.

Rick felt like a fool for being a poor observer. "I didn't notice that."

"Hard to notice at a glance. I helped with the amputation. She'd been shot. Zoos didn't want her. She was going to be destroyed, so I kept her."

"How come somebody shot her?"

"Somebody was an idiot."

Rick appreciated the directness of the answer. "I read in your bird book last night that condors got shot a lot, and poisoned too. Why do people shoot 'em? Because they're vultures?"

"Because large, moving targets are tempting to idiots."

"Why do they poison 'em?"

"They don't. People poison ground squirrels and so on, the condor eats the ground squirrel. . . ."

It was probably the pothunters, Rick thought, that accounted for Lon's bad mood. Plus he had someone in his camp that he had to relate to, and he'd already said he liked to be alone.

"Just one more question. The book called it the California condor. Yesterday you called it the North American condor."

Lon looked up from his scope and said sharply, "Yeah, well, if I ever write the book, it'll get renamed. They used to live even in what's now New York and Florida. Just because their range shrank to California in the last hundred years, that's not a good reason to call it the California condor. What if bald eagles go extinct in the lower forty-eight, and they're only left in Alaska? Should we start calling it the Alaska eagle?"

"I guess not. Sorry I asked so many questions."

Lon wasn't listening. He was pointing his little antenna toward different spots in the cliffs. "I've got a visual on everyone but M4."

Suddenly Lon's radio started beeping, four quick

beats. The pattern kept repeating. "So *there* you are, M4. He's out of sight, all right. Looks like he roosted in the cove north of where the cliff turns the corner."

"You got transmitters on the birds?"

"So we can track 'em with radiotelemetry. There's one transmitter on the wing, along with the tag, and one on the tail. M4's tail transmitter went out on me and I had to replace it. He's awful happy to be out of that pen."

"What pen?"

Lon pointed high above. Rick was surprised to see a structure up there, thirty or forty feet back on the slope from the edge of the cliff, that he'd completely overlooked. It was a large pen, very well camouflaged, with a chain-link fence around it and a roof of camouflage netting. At the back of the pen sat a squat makeshift shelter of plywood painted rusty red like the cliffs.

"The birds were in there for six weeks before we released them," Lon commented. "To get 'em used to their new environment. They'd get so excited seeing the ravens and eagles flying by. . . ."

"So how'd you recapture that M4?"

"With a big net. I released him again last evening right before I drove back down. I hope he behaves himself. I'm not too happy about him roosting last night away from the others."

"How come?"

"They're supposed to be forming a flock. It's crucial for their survival. Funny about M4. The biologists at the L.A. Zoo, where he was hatched, told me he's been a maverick right along—never socialized much with the other juveniles. They thought I might get some unpredictable behavior out of him."

"You oughta call him Maverick instead of M4."

"We don't give 'em those kinds of names."

Rick was surprised at the bite in the man's reaction. He'd said it only in jest. "How come?" he ventured.

"What's going on in that bird's brain isn't vaguely human. That's one of my pet peeves—people assigning human personality characteristics to wild animals."

After a long, silent moment the biologist suddenly changed his tone, apparently working on his head, as he'd put it. "Hey, let's eat some breakfast, and then I can show 'em to you up close. They're due for some more bird feed."

Bird feed, Rick mused. This must be where the dead calves come in.

Over cereal Lon said, "The Humvee went out during the middle of the night."

"Guess I slept through it. They must've retrieved their stash of pottery, right? That must've been what you radioed about last night. Do you think they got busted when they got back to Hanksville?"

"I hope so, but I doubt it. I left a message for a ranger I know at the park. I asked if somebody from the park could initiate a casual stop. I figure chances are fair to good that those guys would have left a glimpse of pottery showing somewhere in that Humvee."

"Couldn't the Park Service get a search warrant?"

"I just told them I had a hunch—not enough to get a warrant."

He didn't tell them about me, Rick realized.

"Probably I shouldn't have done what I did," Lon continued. "If Carlile and Gunderson suspect that somebody's on to them, they might get so cautious they'll never get caught. I was thinking this was the perfect opportunity to catch them by surprise. I just wish I could've reached the Maze ranger personally, instead of relaying a message through someone else."

"Don't you have a cell phone?"

"They don't work out here. Anyway, I'm just happy those two are gone. I need to get back to work."

Lon went to the commissary tent and emerged a minute later with a frozen calf over his shoulder. "Where do you get those things?" Rick asked.

"They're stillborn dairy cattle donated from a farm in Arizona. Hey, you drive."

"Drive? Drive where?"

"Up the dugway, for starters—the switchbacks up to the plateau."

"You're kidding."

"If I remember correctly, that's what you were in the process of doing yesterday morning. You might be helpful around here if you could drive." Lon laid the carcass gently down in the bed of the pickup.

The man was serious. "Show me how," Rick said. "I mean, show me the gears, which one I should really be in. I warn you, though, you're putting your life in shaky hands."

"Life's an adventure. Don't kill me, though."

Shortly past the bend where Lon had stopped him the morning before, the dugway got rough, and steepened. Rick concentrated with all his might as he lurched slowly through potholes and up and over little ledges. He was holding his breath; the consequences of failure were unthinkable. Halfway up, he was about to glance out of the driver's window over the side. "Don't look down," Lon warned him. "That's the trick at first. Your vision will swim and your stomach will go into free fall."

"Gotcha." The truck was creeping up the grade in the lowest of the low-range four-wheel-drive gears. "I could walk up here faster than this," Rick commented.

"Naturally, but our dead friend in the back can't. Unless you wanted to carry him. Hey, you're starting to relax—that's good. It's not as scary as it looks. It's just the exposure that makes it feel that way."

Finally they crested the top of the grade onto the plateau. He'd done it. "How much did we just climb?"

"Eight hundred feet."

Across the flats Lon pointed him onto a dirt track that wound through thickets of pinyon and juniper. After a few minutes they reached a terrace of solid rock. "Park here. We'll leave the bird feed to thaw out for the time being. Grab the binoculars; I'll get the scope. Walk as quiet as you can across this slickrock."

"It doesn't look slick."

"Means smooth. All these smooth sandstone surfaces in this country are called slickrock."

They sneaked among the bushy trees until they came to a plywood blind that had been erected beside a single juniper. Lon tiptoed the last twenty feet through the chalky red dirt with Rick in his footsteps. When Rick brought his eye to one of the holes in the blind he saw three birds out on the slickrock that sloped down toward the edge of the cliffs. One was standing on a carcass and pulling off stringy pieces of meat, while the other two stood off to the side and watched.

Rick could tell immediately that the two waiting their turn were condors. They were very large black birds, easily three feet tall, with long and leathery tapering gray-skinned heads. Their bills were white and convincingly designed for tearing flesh. Like thick stalks, their necks emerged from a spiked ruff of feathers that looked ornamental, like a collar.

When they pulled in their necks, as one of them was doing now, the head rested against the ruff and it appeared that the bird had no neck at all, only a head and shoulders.

The bird on the carcass—it had to be an eagle— was sleek, streamlined, and regal. Its head was covered with golden blond feathers. Watching the smaller bird feed, the condors seemed unsure of themselves. Their circular metal tags attached barely back from the leading edge of each wing identified the birds as M1 and M3.

"Golden eagle on the carcass," Lon whispered. "Two female condors waiting. Odd-numbered condors are females."

M1 was edging closer to the carcass, a little short on the virtue Lon had said was the strong suit of condors. Encouraged, perhaps thinking there was strength in numbers, M3 walked a little closer too. They slouched as they walked, Rick noticed, but that seemed fitting for vultures.

The golden eagle reacted by hissing, then leaping at them with talons outstretched, like a kick boxer. With their immense wings beating in reverse, the condors stepped back just in time. After retreating a little farther, they hissed. The eagle, ripping off another piece of meat, stared at them fiercely.

"Mr. Nice Guy," Rick whispered.

A pair of jet-black ravens landed close by, then hopped and walked to the edge of an invisible circle that the eagle's presence seemed to have drawn around the carcass. After a minute the ravens darted in from different directions. One tried to distract the eagle while the second attempted to rip free some meat. The eagle was too fast for them.

"Are eagles always this ferocious?"

"Depends on the eagle. Usually they tolerate the ravens pretty well."

"Do eagles ever let the condors on the carcass with them?"

"Usually the condors have to wait their turn. These guys seem to know that by instinct. I'm proud of 'em. Their parents never taught 'em that."

Suddenly the eagle flew off. The condors fed for half an hour, then lumbered along the slickrock flapping their wings and made short flights along the edge of the cliff. "Let's plant the new carcass," Lon said.

They placed the new carcass farther to the north, where a pair of junipers served as a natural blind.

"We can watch awhile," the biologist said.

After fifteen minutes a raven showed up. The first thing it did was tear out the calf's eyes. In an hour's time there were six ravens. "They've already opened it up," Lon said. "This is good. Ravens find carcass, condors see ravens, condors find food."

Rick was tiring of the wait. He didn't have a fraction of the patience the biologist had.

Suddenly Lon was pointing. "Look high," he whispered.

A condor was soaring high above the rim.

"Gotta be M4," Lon said. He raised his binoculars. "Definitely is. Come on down, M4, come on down!"

Rick located the bird through the spotting scope. He could see every feather. The condor was holding his position against the wind, broad wings perfectly flat, tail ruddering slightly as it angled its head to look below like a pilot looking out of the cockpit window. "I see what you mean about the magnificent flying machine. That's a spectacular bird."

"Yes, sir, that he is. Come on down, M4. You gotta be hungry. He hasn't eaten since I released him."

"He'll die if he doesn't eat soon?"

"It's not that drastic. A condor can go ten or twelve days."

"How do you know for sure he hasn't eaten? There must have been times you weren't watching."

Lon put his finger to his throat. "They got a pouch in their esophagus that we call the crop in the bird biz. . . . Holds food until they're ready to digest it, or afterward if they're feeding their young. The crop pooches out when it's full."

M4 was turning a circle. Rick lost him in the scope and watched without it. Suddenly there were three more large birds in the air above the rim. "Not eagles, I hope."

"All condors. Look, M4's coming down."

Within a few minutes they were watching four condors at once feeding on the calf. "This is a first!" Lon said, beside himself. "And no eagles in sight. Eat your fill, guys. Car-ry-on."

"I got it. Carry-on, carrion . . ."

"You pounce on a pun like a coyote on a field mouse."

Afterward Lon wanted him to drive back down the grade to camp. "Get some more practice."

This time Rick couldn't help looking down, and he was terrified. "Easy does it," Lon kept saying. "You're concentrating too hard. Enjoy yourself. Everything's fine. That gear's so strong you'll never need to use the brake."

Out Rick's window, it was hundreds and hundreds

of feet down. His vision swam, he felt sick. "If you say so."

"Talk to me."

"You're kidding."

"I'm serious. You'll squeeze that steering wheel to death."

"Okay. . . . Will the condors ever be able to find dead cows on their own . . . without them appearing as if by magic?"

"Sure they will! Canyonlands National Park is surrounded by cattle country for hundreds and hundreds of miles—almost all of it public land with grazing by permit. The ranchers lose two percent of their cattle every year to natural causes. Cattle even graze the meadows on the mountain ranges you see on the horizon. Those mountains will be within easy reach for these condors."

"I don't think I'll look at the horizon."

"Keep your eye on the road, such as it is. In addition to cattle, these condors will find deer, elk, bighorn sheep, jackrabbits, ground squirrels. . . . Everything that lives dies, and it all needs to get cleaned up. The Southwest is going to be Condor Country again!"

"That sounds like great material for a TV ad. Condors might get so popular there'll be a new cigarette brand named after them."

Lon chuckled, and gestured grandly. "I can picture it: a guy on horseback, a condor in flight against a classic canyonlands background. The slogan: COME TO CONDOR COUNTRY. A vulture logo would be *perfect* for cigarettes. No warning from the surgeon general necessary on a pack of condors!"

"Light up a Condor! Or try our new menthol Condors—for that refreshing taste of the Ice Age!" To

Rick's immense relief, they were almost down off the grade.

Lon was still chuckling as they pulled into camp. "Con-dors . . . you too can become carrion!"

Rick turned off the ignition. His T-shirt was drenched with sweat.

10

Rick was having the flying dream again. The Maze was spread out below him, the entire labyrinth of twisting canyons. From the air it didn't look intimidating at all. In fact, it made a pattern, it made sense. He was learning the secrets of all the hidden, intricate canyons, one after the next. Every single dead end was revealed for what it was.

Off to his right a dark shape was coming to join him: another flier. It was a bird, a very large dark bird.

One of the condors, he realized. It looked primitive, prehistoric, almost like a pterodactyl. Wing tip to wing tip, they left the Maze behind and flew out over the open ocean. His fingers were almost touching the condor's outspread flight feathers. His eye met the eye of the condor. The bird's eye was red.

Someone was trying to call him down by singing,

strangely enough. He couldn't make out the words, but he knew he couldn't land on the water. Panicky, he looked all around, beginning to doubt that he could fly. The condor was gone and land was nowhere in sight.

The voice, however, was still there. Someone was singing in a deep, booming, reassuring voice.

"Buffalo gals, won't you come out tonight,
Come out tonight, come out tonight . . .''

The song kept cutting through. Rick struggled to consciousness, toward that voice like a life buoy. He remembered that baritone. It went with the man with the beard. It was Lon.

"Buffalo gals, won't you come out tonight,
Come out tonight, come out tonight,
Buffalo gals, won't you come out tonight,
And dance by the light of the moon.''

Dawn was breaking. "What's going on?" Rick groaned.

"Wake-up call for my driver!"

"You're kidding."

"Pull on your clothes! I got the truck packed!"

Packed for what? Rick thought. He reached for his jeans and some of the underwear Lon had allocated him.

Lon sang another round of "Buffalo Gals" while Rick was pulling on his socks and his shoes. He reached for his flannel shirt and stumbled outside. The first light was illuminating the red cliffs above camp. "Where we going?" Rick managed.

"You're still asleep. I'll do the driving on the way up. Here, put this on."

Lon handed him an oversize glove. Rick yawned. "What's this for?"

Lon explained that they were taking the eagle with them, and Rick's forearm was going to be its perch.

Rick was wide-awake now. "You're kidding! You want me to hold the eagle?"

A few minutes later he was seated in the truck with the bald eagle on his left forearm. The eagle's face was just inches from his. "What if she pecks my eye out?"

"You'd be the first."

Lon had strapped one of the long plastic tubes from behind the tents across the top of the camper shell. Out in front of the truck cab it was supported by a T-shaped bracket attached to the front bumper. Lon was being very mysterious. Rick guessed they were going up onto the plateau to erect an antenna. "So what's this all about?" he asked.

"I need you to drive back down. I don't get to do this except when Josh or some of the others are here, or unless I want to do some serious walking afterward. It's one of the disadvantages to working alone."

As they crested the grade, Lon turned off the road to the left and parked on a big patch of slickrock only a hundred feet or so from the edge of the cliff. Rick stood by with the eagle while the biologist unloaded the long plastic tube from the truck. Then Lon pulled out a long, furled bundle of bright red, blue, and white material wrapped around long aluminum tubes.

Wrong about the antenna. "Umbrella?" Rick ventured. "Giant beach umbrella?"

Lon looked up with a quick smile. "Nope. Hang glider."

"Really? Is it yours?"

"Sure."

Lon was working fast, unfolding the aluminum members of the glider, attaching guy wires, sliding extremely thin metal ribs into sleeves in the wing.

Rick shivered. The day was only starting to warm up. "You're really going to jump off this cliff?"

"Run off. I haven't had many chances since I got here. I took Josh up a couple of weeks ago in my tandem glider. Andrea's been up too. She works with Josh."

"You don't expect me to—"

"Don't worry, this is my solo glider. You're gonna drive the truck down to the LZ—the landing zone. Right now you can take Sky over to that bracket on the front of the truck. She'll step off your arm."

The eagle stepped to the bracket just as Lon had said she would. Sky looked around fiercely, opened her wings to the wind, the good one and the stub, and started flapping in place.

Lon was walking close to the edge of the cliff. Rick tried to follow but could feel himself hanging back. Lon reached into his back pocket and pulled out a length of neon-green surveying tape. He stepped forward to the very edge, knelt, and tied it to a dead branch on a stunted juniper. "Indicates wind direction," he explained. "I need a good strong wind blowing directly at me. If it's coming from the side—no good."

The tape fluttered smartly in the wind. "Perfect," Lon said. "Mornings are excellent this time of year. It only takes an hour or so for the sun to warm up this east-facing cliff. Warm air rises up the cliffs. Until October cools off some more, mornings are best. Once the sun has a chance to cook all this rock out here, it creates thermals strong enough to yank you into heaven."

Lon pointed below. "See the road running by those buttes?"

"I see it."

"All together, the buttes are called Standing Rocks, but each one has its own name. Closest to us is the Wall. The huge one, shaped kind of like the Sphinx, is called Lizard Rock for some reason. The Plug's out there past it, then Chimney Rock."

"Chimney Rock is obvious."

"Okay, follow the road down to the huge field in between the sand dunes and the Doll House down at the end of the road."

"I see the field. I drove all the way to that Doll House when I took off with your truck. It looked more like a bunch of giants to me."

"The field is my primary LZ. That's where you pick me up—you'll see the flags. I need to land into the wind."

"One thing I don't understand."

"Name it."

"Why did we bring the eagle with us?"

"Oh. Sky's going with me."

"You're kidding."

"It's the only way she can fly these days."

Rick was having a hard time believing all this. First the hang glider, then the eagle . . . "How long have you been flying hang gliders?"

"Twenty-one years."

"So it's safe."

"Depends on the pilot, depends on conditions. The way I look at it, it's safer than driving on a freeway with drunks and homicidal maniacs."

"Actually," Rick admitted, "I had a flying dream last night."

Lon's eyes lit up. "As in . . . flying like a bird? Tell me about it."

Rick shrugged. "I was flying with one of your condors. Over the Maze."

Lon clapped him on the shoulder. "A man after my own heart."

"Do you ever have flying dreams?"

"All the time, but now they're hang gliding dreams. When I was a kid I would kind of hover with my arms out wide. All the wings I needed were my outstretched arms."

"Were people always motioning for you to come down?"

"All the time. They thought I was going to crash. They couldn't believe I could really fly."

"What do those flying dreams mean? Is it an escape fantasy? Is it *dying,* and leaving everybody behind?"

"Heard both of those. I've also heard it's about how we puny humans keep searching for the meaning of life. I've heard just about everything. But I have my own theory: flying dreams signify the desire to fly! Since people have had imaginations, they've envied birds. In their dreams they do something about it! Say, would you put the glove back on and bring Sky?"

Lon darted around to the back of the pickup, fished a duffel bag and a helmet from the camper shell. A minute later he was stepping through the leg straps of a full-body harness and passing his arms through the shoulder straps. The harness was a synthetic cocoon that ran from his shoulders to his feet.

"What's in the big pouch over your chest?" Rick asked.

"Parachute," Lon replied with a grin.

Delicately the man positioned the eagle inside an intricate harness of her own. Obviously handmade, the harness left the eagle's head, wings, tail, and feet free. Lon proceeded to wrap each of the eagle's talons with adhesive foam strips. "For my protection—she'll kind of be on my back."

"I don't believe this," Rick said. He was trying to hold the eagle up by the harness strap. Sky was flapping her enormous wing, ready and anxious to fly. She was too heavy for Rick to hold her up for long. He lowered her gently to the ground until her feet found the slickrock.

Lon slipped on his sunglasses, pulled his helmet over his head. It had wraparound jaw protection that momentarily pushed his beard in the wrong direction.

"Hook in," Rick heard the man remind himself. Lon reached over his shoulder and attached his harness, with a carabiner, to the keel of the hang glider above.

"Hook Sky," Lon said. Rick reached in with the bird under the leading edge of the wing. Lon had a carabiner waiting and hooked her in. He screwed the carabiner's locking mechanism down tight.

The man studied the green tape waving in the wind at the edge of the cliff. He took a deep breath, pulled on gloves, then lifted the glider by the two shiny aluminum tubes descending from a common point above him where they were attached to the keel. A thinner bar connected them horizontally, forming a triangle. A small instrument box was attached to the horizontal bar.

There was so much Rick wanted to ask, but this wasn't the time. "Have a good one," he said.

"Thanks."

Rick thought Lon was set to go, but then the man set the glider down on the tiny wheels at the ends of its horizontal bar. "I left the two-way radio in the truck tuned to the frequency of the receiver built into my helmet. All you have to do is push the talk button on the side of the mike when you want to talk."

"Where's yours?"

"On my glove finger here. I can hit it with my thumb. See this wire running up my neck? See where it's jacked into the helmet? I'll let you know if I change my mind about my LZ. You let me know if there's any breaking news back on earth. Stand back, Rick, nice and clear."

Rick walked halfway to the edge of the cliff and stepped away from the runway. He wanted a good look at this.

Lon lifted the glider once again. *"Clear!"* he yelled, and began to jog behind the aluminum triangle.

Rick saw the exact moment of liftoff. Lon's churning legs suddenly left the ground, and he quickly dropped his hands from the near-vertical members of the triangle to the horizontal bar connecting them below. Almost simultaneously he kicked his feet into the bottom of the harness bag and assumed a perfectly prone position. The eagle was perched on his back with her one wing held out and carving the wind.

Lon flew out from the cliff and then up, up, in great spiraling circles. Rick could see him controlling the glider by shifting his weight from side to side or forward and back.

Rick heard the eagle scream. "Unbelievable," he

said under his breath, and then he cheered, and cheered again at the top of his lungs.

He'd never seen anything so beautiful in his life as this man-kite soaring untethered above the canyon-lands. He realized there were tears streaming down his face.

A few minutes later he was back in the truck. Through the windshield, he still had the glider in sight. Several ravens were performing acrobatic maneuvers very close to the glider.

Rick switched on the two-way, picked up the mike, and hit the talk button. "Lon and Sky," he said, "do you read me? Over . . ."

He let his thumb off the button.

"Ten-four. Read you loud and clear. What's up? Over . . ."

"You are. What's the deal with the ravens off your starboard wing? Over . . ."

"Those guys? Just a couple of local pilots."

11

Lon was stuffing the hang glider back in its tube as a white pickup appeared at the edge of the landing zone. The round emblem on its door set Rick's heart pounding. Panicky, he looked to Lon for reassurance.

"Maze ranger," Lon explained. "Park Service. Don't worry. Just don't talk. Don't say anything unless you have to."

The truck pulled to a stop. A man with neatly combed gray hair and a trim gray mustache got out from behind the wheel.

Rick couldn't see the man's eyes behind his sunglasses, but he felt them scrutinizing him. The park ranger looked from Rick to the eagle perched on the carrying bracket at the front of Lon's truck, then back to Rick. Rick tried to quiet his heart.

The nameplate over the man's chest pocket said

JOE PHIPPS. The ranger and the condor biologist shook hands. Rick sidled away and stood by the eagle.

The ranger asked if Lon had taken the eagle flying that morning; Lon said he had. The ranger shook his head, marveling. He glanced at Rick once more, but he didn't say anything.

The ranger started to talk about the weather. He said that the monsoon rains were long overdue. Lon said he expected they were still coming. The ranger asked about the condors. Lon reported that they were doing well.

With another glance in Rick's direction, the ranger said, "Good, I'm really happy to hear that."

"You got my message?" Lon asked.

"Sure did . . . haven't wanted to radio you back on it. As we both know, there's a lot of people listening in on the airwaves. Your message—at least the way it was relayed to me—was mighty cryptic, Lon. I wasn't able to cover the situation myself, but the sheriff covered it for me. The only Humvee that came off the Maze road was driven by Nuke Carlile, and it turns out he's an old friend of the sheriff's."

Lon flinched. "Great, just great. I suppose the sheriff didn't happen to see any artifacts sticking out of the Humvee."

"I don't expect he nosed around much. What did you have to go on, Lon? You see something yourself?"

Lon shook his head. He looked disgusted. "Just a hunch," he said. "A very strong hunch."

At this the ranger's questioning eyes left the biologist and fastened on Rick. Rick was sure the man was guessing that Lon wasn't telling the full story on account of him.

The ranger glanced back at Lon. "I was about to

come see you anyway. I wanted to tell you in person that I've been transferred. All the way up to Oregon."

"I'm sorry to hear that."

"Came up quick. A man in a crucial job at Crater Lake took sick. The position of Maze ranger is sort of in limbo until they build a new station or bring in a portable. It's true I can't patrol the Maze very well from the Island in the Sky. It might be fifteen air miles—"

Lon laughed. "And two hundred some in your truck."

"My kidneys won't miss this excuse for a road. Over the last eleven years I've had my internal organs rearranged for life. I should donate my body to science."

"I'll miss you, Joe. You were a big supporter for the Condor Project coming in here."

The park ranger looked wistfully toward the Doll House. "I'm gonna miss this country. And to tell you the truth, I'm a little concerned about leaving you out here without anyone to check in on you besides your own people."

"How's that, Joe?"

"If the sheriff mentioned your name to Carlile . . ."

"How could that have happened? Why would he do a thing like that?"

"I'm not saying he did, Lon. I just wish I'd known beforehand that they were friends. I could see he wasn't going to do a thing unless he had a name to attach to the accusation."

"My fault. I should've seen this coming."

"You've met Nuke, I take it?"

"He already wasn't very happy to see me in here."

"To my mind—don't quote me on this—he's a classic government hater, and I wouldn't be surprised if he associates you with the government. You know, I tried once to reason with him about Canyonlands National Park belonging to all the people of the United States. About people agreeing that a few places should be left natural, and that's what the national parks are all about."

"I don't suppose that went over too big."

"Nuke said to me, 'It's not the people we're talking about here, it's the *government.*' What can you say to a guy who's consumed by hatred for the government?"

Lon just shrugged.

"After a certain point, hate becomes a brain disease. It distorts a person's perception of reality."

"What's his beef?"

The ranger grinned. "You just said the word. Decades ago Nuke was the rancher who had the grazing permit on this whole district. He's the one who scratched the road in here, for cattle. It was always worse than marginal grazing, but he had a permit on a hundred square miles in here, including the Maze. Of course it was public land even back then, administered by the federal government, but once it became part of the national park, his grazing permit was revoked."

"Amazing to think anyone could've grazed cattle in the Maze."

"There were just enough pockets of grass, especially on the canyon bottoms. Nuke drove cattle into nearly every canyon in the Maze."

"I've seen a few stone staircases . . . knew they were overbuilt for foot traffic."

"Nuke built those stone by stone. Jasper Canyon was the only one he could never manage to drive his cattle into, which is partly why we closed it a few years ago."

"I hadn't heard about that. You mean Jasper is closed to hikers even?"

Jasper, Rick thought. Did Carlile name his pit bull after that canyon?

"That's right. We posted a sign at the trailhead—there's only one path to the bottom, so it was easy to post. We want to have one canyon—for study—that has never been grazed and won't get the hiking traffic in the future that the rest will. Jasper's the closest thing we have to a pristine canyon ecosystem. The idea is to be able to compare all those other canyons with Jasper in order to monitor their recovery from the old grazing damage and the impacts of the new recreational use. If you need to go into Jasper on account of your birds, though, don't worry about it. I'll put a memo to that effect in the file before I leave. Anyway, now you know the story on Carlile."

Lon shook his head. "Still nursing his wounds over that revoked permit, sounds like."

"You and I know that cattle are awfully hard on these arid lands out here, but this didn't make a bit of sense to Carlile. You could tell he'd started thinking of all this country out here as his own property rather than the public's. I'm sure he felt like he was being robbed of what was rightfully his."

"Somehow I can picture him harboring a grudge for a quarter of a century."

"He was offered a permit on higher-quality grazing land of greater acreage, but he wouldn't take it. National Park people bent over backward trying to accommodate him, but for Nuke it was the Maze district or nothing, so it turned out to be nothing. He moved into Moab after that, went to work at the uranium mill. Then just a few years ago he moved back to Hanksville, bought the gas station, and you know the rest."

"It sure would all fit together, him pothunting in here, if I'm right about that. He probably thinks he's just evening up the score, making money on the Maze without working a single cow."

"Just between you and me and the fencepost, I'm standing here rethinking that fire that burned down the ranger station last spring. They never found what caused it. In addition to despising the federal government, Nuke would've had an immediate motive for arson: nobody on the road to take note of his pothunting trips. If that's what happened, it worked. Got me out of his way. All of this is wild conjecture, though, unless you've actually got something on him."

"No, I don't. Just some suspicious behavior. At any rate, I have reason to believe he'll lay off this area now. He was in here night before last, and I'm assuming he pulled out everything he had hidden away. He's too exposed now with me so close. I don't think he'll be back."

"All the same, keep a watchful eye out—" Suddenly the park ranger nodded in Rick's direction. "So who's your shy friend over here?"

"My nephew. My nephew Rick."

"Happy to meet you, Rick. Where you from?"

"California," he answered slowly.

"Oh, whereabouts?"

"Fort Bragg."

"Sure, on the Mendocino coast. My, that's beautiful country. So what do you think of this out here? Couldn't be more different, eh?"

"That's for sure." Rick breathed easier. He was

going to get through this. He was surprised that Lon
had lied for him.

A minute later the park ranger's 4x4 was disap-
pearing up the road. Lon said, "So now we get a bit of
autobiography. You're from Fort Bragg?"

"I'm from a lot of places."

For a moment it looked as if Lon would ask him to
tell more. Rick might have been willing, but the
moment passed. "I'm hungry," Lon said. "How about
you?"

It was midmorning when they got back to camp.
Rick ate cold cereal with strawberries, a cup of yogurt,
two bagels with cream cheese. Lon nibbled his three
cold hot dogs as he made observations through the
spotting scope and jotted down notes. Rick said,
"Have you ever tried cooking those?"

"More trouble than it's worth," came the gruff
response.

Sometimes Lon could look so tough. It wasn't just
the scar, it was his entire body language. He wasn't
someone you'd want to have for an enemy. "Aren't
those tube steaks supposed to be bad for you? I mean,
all those preservatives?"

"I figure I'll be so well preserved I'll live forever."

"Condiments? Ever try condiments? You know,
like mustard?"

"No point in gilding the lily. Less is more."

Lon's philosophy, Rick thought. He wondered if
Lon had ever owned a house, or how long it had been
since he'd even lived in one.

Lon never looked away from his scope while he
was talking, which made it easier to ask him questions. "What would you think if I took a hike in the
Maze sometime?"

The biologist turned from the scope, speared him

with those penetrating blue eyes. "What am I all of a sudden, your parent? Your guardian or something?"

"I didn't—"

"Hey, I'm just a guy out here doing his job. If you want to hang out here awhile, that's okay. I thought you had that figured out."

"Got it," Rick said, squaring his shoulders.

He nursed his wounds in his tent. Lon just wanted to be left alone with his condors.

Rick couldn't help it, he'd started to care about the condors himself. Maybe because they were outcasts and the odds were all against them.

Rick couldn't help that he'd started to care about the man too, whatever his real name was—even if he *was* damaged somehow and more than a little strange. The man and the birds and Rick Walker, they were all damaged goods.

And why *had* he asked Lon's permission to hike in the Maze?

Rick nodded off and slept until the tent canvas, whipping with the wind, woke him up. He went back outside, not knowing what to expect.

Lon was still seated on his lawn chair facing the cliffs. The clouds had grown tall and dark, and the wind was starting to blow hard. Rick wondered what rain would look like in these canyonlands of solid rock.

Two of the condors were hanging in the sky a hundred feet or so above the rim, like kites. Lon reached for his binoculars.

A third condor took to the air, joined them, then shot away from the red cliffs in the direction of the camp. The condor was passing directly overhead. Rick noticed the flat, stable plane of its wings. Unlike the turkey vultures he remembered from California, the condor flew without rocking or tilting. A supreme flier, that's what it was. He could see the long individual feathers extending from the wing tips like fingers. As the huge bird soared by, a musical whistling sound took Rick completely by surprise.

"M4," Lon muttered. "Turn back, you goof, turn back."

The condor flapped its wings once and kept soaring over the open country in the direction of Lizard Rock.

"Come down, come down!"

The condor soared high over the squatting monumental butte. It kept on flying past the spire of Chimney Rock, where it disappeared from view.

"What's the deal?" Rick asked.

There was a mix of admiration and disappointment on Lon's face. "Maverick's just made it tough on himself."

Maverick? Rick thought. Lon just called one of his condors by a nickname. My nickname.

Rick thought better of mentioning it. Instead he said, "The sound that his wings made . . . "

"I call that condor music."

The mercurial biologist was unmistakably trying to be friendly.

"So what do you do now?"

"We track him with the radio. This is all in the game. This is what makes it interesting."

12

Past the Standing Rocks they jumped out of the truck. Lon held up the small tracking antenna while tuning in the condor's frequency on the radio fastened to his belt. He pointed the antenna north, toward the Maze, then rotated it gradually to the east.

Four rapid beeps started to come in, then grew stronger and stronger as the antenna pointed straight down the road. "That's good," Lon said. "He's landed. If we're lucky, he won't have landed somewhere real tricky."

They drove another half mile, took another reading. Lon scanned ahead with his powerful binoculars but couldn't see Maverick. "How much do we have on the odometer?"

"Four and a half miles."

"The dope."

"You have to hand it to him, though. From what you're saying, that's a pretty amazing flight for his age."

"An epic flight. But there's a reason we pick a line of cliffs for our reintroduction sites. There are thermal upcurrents along the cliffs that provide tremendous lift. Fledglings can fly back and forth along the rim for weeks as they improve their flying skills. Even without parents to teach them, fledgling condors tend to be canny enough to stick with the good flying air and all those safe perches that the cliffs provide. It's real different down on the flats. Even an adult condor has to work like crazy to get airborne off level ground."

"You mean he might not be able to get back up?"

"Might not. He won't be the only one to go through this lesson; he's just the first. Let's drive a little farther, see if we can spot him."

They did spot him, out in the middle of Lon's landing zone.

Lon passed the binoculars to Rick. The condor was looking all around like a lost kid in the big city. "He looks clueless," Rick said.

"He may be an orphan, but he's got some instincts. He's been looking at this landscape for six weeks. He knows that those cliffs back there are home base."

They waited for the condor's next move. They waited all afternoon through the building of the clouds, through thunder and lightning and rain lashing the windshield. Maverick, standing in the rain, was a murky and forlorn figure.

"Won't he catch sick?" Rick worried.

"Condors are tough, tough birds. They're going to be out here in the winter, in the cold and snow. Sometimes they'll move to a protected spot, but a lot of times they won't."

"It snows out here?"

"Not a lot, but it does."

"You'll be here in the winter?"

"Sure. If this first year is successful, I might be here year-round for the next twenty. More birds twice a year, same as at Vermilion Cliffs, in Arizona, and our California sites."

"Vermilion Cliffs—is that where Josh comes from?"

Lon nodded. "North of the Grand Canyon and southwest of Page, Arizona. Josh and Andrea and David work there; I used to. It's our third year down there—fledged twenty-eight birds so far."

Rick thought about the big net in the back of the truck. "It's five-thirty. What if it gets dark? Aren't you going to try to catch him?"

"Not today. Let's hope he gets anxious with the dark coming on and flies to his familiar roosts. It's best if he does it on his own. My chances of netting him in the open on the LZ are about zip anyway. I don't want to spook him into some worse spot than he is now. Better to wait, let him rest, see if he can possibly take off cleanly, gain some altitude, head home. I wouldn't put it past him. He's the most precocious flier of any condor fledgling I've ever seen."

"Sounds like you think he can do it."

"I think he's got it in him. He's got some serious flaws, but he's also got great potential if he just survives the next couple months."

They watched until dark. Maverick never flew. "What now?"

"We hope for the best," Lon said grimly. "We'll be back at first light. Hope the coyotes don't get him."

"He's awful big. Can't he fight 'em off with his

talons, like that eagle did to M1 and M3?"

"Condors aren't raptors—aren't designed to kill. Their feet are different. They can hiss and grunt and put up a good bluff beating their wings, but when it comes down to it, their safety depends on flying. That's why they need to roost every night in a place predators can't reach, where they'll be able to lift off easily too."

They returned to camp. Lon verified that the rest of the condors were accounted for. They'd perched close to one another as usual, in a draw below the Needle carcass, named after a nearby pinnacle. "Let's have a real meal," Lon announced. "We've got a lot of fresh food, and that's not going to be the case much longer. All this salad stuff, some steaks . . ."

"You're kidding."

"All wrapped up nice in the bottom drawer of the fridge. Last time I fed 'em to the condors, when the birds were still in the pen. Made a nice treat."

"How do they like their steaks?"

"On the raw side. Yourself?"

"Medium rare."

"If you think about it, humans are vultures too. We locate our carrion at the supermarket."

"If you're trying to gross me out of my steak, forget it."

"I'll warm up some beans. You're on for salad."

"How should we cook the steaks?"

"I always hold mine over an open fire with my hands. That's why I don't eat steak very often. If you've got a better idea, you're in charge."

"Let's just kind of sear 'em in the frying pan." Rick found a pan, lit the burner. "Hey," he called. "What about Sky? Maybe she'd like to join us. I bet she'd appreciate a big, bloody steak. What do you say?"

That caught Lon's fancy. "I usually feed her out behind the tents, but sure, let's invite her to dinner." Lon got his glove, went out back, and returned with the eagle on his arm. "I think she'd like hers rare," he said, setting Sky down on the slickrock.

Soon the three of them were gnashing at their bloody steaks by the light of a propane lantern. There was no more talk of Maverick. Tomorrow would be here soon enough.

13

"Is it morning?" Rick asked.

"Close enough. Let's go."

Maverick had flown, but in the wrong direction. They located him perched on top of one of the giants in the Doll House. "We can't afford to spook him," Lon said. "If he flies any farther east, over the river, I doubt very much we'll ever see him again. He's definitely not ready for a major flight over a bottomless drop like that."

"When would he be?"

"Couple of months, maybe. There's a lot to learn. Six or eight months from now, a hundred and fifty miles in a day would be no problem. Up to fifteen thousand feet in altitude, no problem."

"Don't let him hear you. How long could he sit there?"

"Maybe he'll take some short hops. It's possible he won't make a move until he's hungry again. I don't know what he's going to do."

They returned to camp. Lon had fallen silent. Rick could tell that he was less and less optimistic about Maverick.

Lon turned to observing the others. By late morning the five were flying up and down the line of cliffs. Two landed by the new Double Juniper carcass. An aggressive golden eagle, possibly the one they'd seen close up from the blind, wouldn't let them feed.

Lon scribbled notes furiously, then started pecking out an official-looking report on his manual typewriter. He explained that each day he provided a summary of the birds' behavior and activities. "I'm typing up yesterday's report right now. It's my longest one yet, on account of Maverick."

"Who reads 'em?"

"Anyone who's interested. People really like these field notes. They go out all over the country on the Internet."

"The Condor Project has a home page?"

"Sure, like everybody else these days. Josh takes out my notes and updates the Maze site. After his next visit he'll enter all this stuff. A couple of weeks from now, kids in schools all around the country will be reading about Maverick's epic flight and misadventure."

"Do they see pictures of the condors?"

"Sure. Andrea took lots of pictures the day we released 'em."

"Is there a picture of you?"

Lon snorted. He thought that was funny. Something on the cliffs caught his eye; he reached for the binoculars. An eagle was dive-bombing a condor that was flying a hundred feet or so above the rim. The young condor maneuvered well enough to avoid being struck, then found a safe perch in the cliffs. A short while later it happened again.

"I'm getting pretty bent out of shape about the eagles," Rick said.

"Don't," Lon told him. "It's all a part of a condor's education."

They drove back to the Doll House. Maverick had flown onto the flats among the formations. The flats were sprinkled with sagebrush, cactus, huge boulders, and numbers of pinyons and junipers—lots of hiding places for coyotes, according to Lon. "I can't risk him spending another night out in the open. I'm not going to lose that bird."

"You're going to try to net him?"

Stroking his beard thoughtfully, Lon nodded.

For more than thirty minutes Rick watched Lon inching on his elbows and belly toward the condor. The net was nearly three feet in diameter, like a huge fishing net. Thirty feet remained between the man and the bird, with only open ground between them. Just when it seemed this would go on forever, Rick detected a quick motion of the condor's head in Lon's direction. The bird was on to him. Suddenly Lon rose and started sprinting.

Maverick was hopping and then running as fast as he could, beating his great wings. Rick was amazed by his size, by his speed as well. Lon was running full out and was very close to being close enough to net the bird. With a horizontal leap, Lon lunged and came up with only air. Rick watched as Maverick, wings beating furiously, gradually gained altitude and flew off.

"That was quite a chase," Rick said afterward. "You've got serious roadburn on your arms there."

"Where'd he go?"

"North."

"Maverick's really spooked now. I must've been an awful scary sight. We're going to have to try a different approach."

"Disguise yourself as a dead cow?"

"Sort of," Lon said, but he didn't explain. "Let's see if we can get another visual on him."

On foot now, they followed the signal from Lon's electronic bloodhound north toward the confluence of the two rivers. The standing formations surrounding them were fantastic beyond imagining. It was a broken country of slickrock domes and terraces, cactus flats, and stone arches. Monumental sandstone fins stood in perfectly parallel rows with slots of flat, shady ground in between.

The signal was strong but twilight was fading. Finally Lon located the condor on top of one of the narrow fins.

Rick set up the spotting scope. Maverick had already tucked his head away in the ruff on his shoulders. "I'm going to catch you, Maverick," Lon muttered.

The man's eyes were ablaze with determination. "We have a lot of work to do, Rick. Hang the field glasses from the scope; we'll leave them here. We'll have to find this place in the dark. When we find the equipment, we'll know we're back at the right place. We'll have plenty to carry as it is: a shovel and a bow saw, some plastic buckets, a propane lantern, bird feed. . . . Let's get going!"

14

They took their positions half an hour before dawn.
The rest was waiting.

Starting with first light, Rick had the binoculars on
the condor. He saw the bird bring its head out from
behind its shoulders and start looking around. From
the cover of a slab of rock and through the gap in the
branches of a juniper, Rick observed every slight
movement, hoping Maverick was about to fly.

He let his mind drift, imagining what that might be
like. To fly, to be actually flying. To be soaring above
these endless canyons and seeing it all from the air. To
fly like Maverick, or like Lon under his hang glider.
Lon had mentioned taking people up tandem. Rick
could almost imagine what that would be like, the two
of them under that big wing.

If Lon ever offered, he wasn't going to say no. Even

if he was afraid. If he could take that leap off the cliff, he'd be living his dream.

The first pair of ravens flew to the carcass in mid-morning. Maverick looked on as the ravens started with the calf's eyes, then opened the belly. By noon they'd been joined by a dozen others. One o'clock, one-thirty, and still the condor hadn't flown. It took the patience of a vulture to wait out a vulture.

He wondered if it was hot in the pit. He wondered if Lon was all cramped up. He wondered if the man was trying to remain in a kneeling position all this time, the way he'd been when Rick had left him before dawn.

He was proud of that pit and the camouflage job they had done. There wasn't a bit of raw earth showing around it. They'd hauled off every bucketful and scattered it. If the ravens hadn't been suspicious, then Maverick shouldn't be either.

Maybe Maverick just wasn't hungry?

It was just after 2:00 P.M. when Rick saw the sudden bend in the bird's knees, saw him unfold his great wings and launch himself off the edge of the fin. Maverick was coming down to feed! Rick saw him put his tail flaps down, flare his wings, and make a less than graceful landing fifteen feet from the carcass.

The ravens were agitated by the condor's arrival, but they didn't fly. Maverick acted like a spectator for a full ten minutes before he made his move. Slouching close to the pit, he thrust his head forward, hissing. The ravens stayed by the calf until Maverick bluffed with several rapid flaps of his huge wings, which scattered them.

Looking around carefully, the condor stepped onto the calf. He continued looking around a full minute

longer before he began to feed. At this exact moment
Lon was looking up from underneath Maverick and
the calf, through the slot they'd so carefully camouflaged with weeds and bits of grass. At this moment
Lon was looking right at the condor's face as the bird
bobbed for meat.

The wait continued. It was killing Rick that the
biologist hadn't made his move. If Lon waited much
longer, Maverick might step off the carcass. Maverick
might fill his crop and be gone.

The ravens were moving back in, working at the
calf around the edges. The condor lunged at one;
it jumped away. Maverick shifted his position, and
started looking around warily instead of feeding.

That's when Lon struck. Through the binoculars
Rick saw it clearly. He saw Lon's hands seize the base
of the condor's legs. Suddenly the condor was wearing leg shackles made of human hands.

Rick expected that the condor would slash instantly at the man's hands with his powerful beak, but
Maverick hesitated, as if his feet were stuck in place
of their own accord. He beat his great wings once,
twice, trying to rise, then flapped for balance as Lon
began to pull him slowly downward.

As the condor was descending, it folded its wings
tight against its body as if cooperating. Rick watched
as Maverick's shoulders and head slowly disappeared
inside the pit.

And then Rick ran. He ran as fast as he could.

"What can I do?" he asked, all out of breath.

"Lay the calf aside," came the voice from inside the
pit. "Clear off the branches and stuff, but not too fast.
Easy does it."

Within a few minutes Rick cleared most of the roof

from the pit. Lon was kneeling with the body of the condor under his left arm, his right hand holding Maverick's head and jaw from underneath so the bird couldn't attack him. Lon rose slowly until he was standing upright. "Man, am I sore."

"Good job!" Rick cried. He'd never felt so happy in his life. It was amazing to see the condor up close. Incredible. So prehistoric-looking, so strange. Maverick's feet were enormous.

"I need a step," Lon said calmly. "Slide down into the pit, Rick, real slow. I'll use your back."

It worked. Lon stepped out of the pit without stumbling or jostling the bird. "Wait a minute," Rick said. "We forgot the bird kennel. We've got nothing to carry him in."

"Get me that red jacket of yours. If he's wrapped up he won't be as nervous. I thought about the bird kennel and decided against it. We're close enough we don't need it. Too much risk of Maverick injuring himself banging around in there loose, after being so stressed out."

Rick ran for his jacket, helped maneuver it around the bird as Lon readjusted the grip of his left arm.

"Okay," Lon announced. "Let's march. Bring the binoculars; we'll come back for the spotting scope and the rest of the stuff later."

Rick didn't say another word until they got back to the truck. Lon was all concentration, walking with the bird, and there was a painful grimace on his face. "My arm's all cramped up," he said finally. "We're going to have to transfer him to you."

"I'm not sure I can do it."

Lon shook his head. "Set that stuff aside, open up the passenger door, and get into the seat. I'm going to

give him to you. I want you to swivel toward me as I
come to you. Take hold of the bird exactly as I'm holding him right now. Left arm first; I'll pull mine away
when yours is in place. Then we'll make the switch
with our right hands. Hold him firm against yourself
so he's got no room to maneuver, but not so tight you
hurt him. Stay focused. And don't be afraid of holding
his head firm. If his head gets loose, he could put your
eye out."

"Got it." Rick's heart was racing.

The transfer went as smoothly as Lon had planned
it. Rick couldn't believe that he was holding this huge
bird. The condor's head was right next to his.

Lon slid into the driver's seat. "Maverick looks a
little silly in that jacket of yours."

"He's not fighting it."

"He's terrified, but he knows he's caught. This is
when that legendary condor patience kicks in."

Then they were under way. This was the strangest
experience of Rick's life. The condor's leathery head
was in Rick's right hand, and the bird kept looking at
him with his red eye. The bird would blink, but not
with an eyelid like a human eyelid. It was more like
the shutter of a camera set at the fastest possible
speed.

Rick's left hand was planted on the condor's
breastbone. He could feel the condor's heart beating,
so fast it was alarming. "His heart's going berserk,"
Rick warned. "I can feel it."

With a smile the biologist said, "That's part of
why they can fly. Maverick's heart rate is a lot
faster than yours and mine. Think about a hum-
mingbird's."

Lon didn't stop at camp. He drove up the switchbacks. He drove as gently as possible, but there was no alternative to lurching through the potholes and up and over the steplike ledges. Rick braced with his feet spread wide while pushing hard against the seat back.

At last they topped out and turned off the road. A few minutes later, his responsibility was almost over. Lon shut the truck down, came around, and opened the passenger door. He led Rick around the junipers and across the slickrock to the back of the release pen where the birds had spent their first six weeks at the Maze site.

Lon opened the door of the pen; Rick stepped inside. Lon closed the door behind him. "Step into the daylight, a little farther into the pen," Lon said. "Then kneel down slowly on one knee. We want him to see where he is for half a minute so he doesn't go crashing into the fence when you let him go."

Rick knelt. "How do I let him go?"

"Both hands at once. Just kind of give him a little toss, jacket and all."

Rick did exactly as he'd been instructed. The condor burst out of the jacket, ran with beating wings to the far end of the pen. "Back in the slammer for this juvenile delinquent," Rick said. "You're busted, Maverick."

"Hey, this is supposed to be home. It's just until he cools his jets and gets his bearings again."

"I wasn't really thinking about him, I guess," Rick admitted. He looked Lon in the eyes. "That's what's going to happen to me."

Rick saw it in the man's reaction, the kindness underneath the scar.

"It's time for us to talk," Lon said.

Rick put two fingers gently to the wound over his own cheekbone. It wasn't pounding so much anymore. A hard scab had formed.

He took a breath. "I escaped from Blue Canyon Youth Detention Center outside Las Vegas, Nevada."

"That's a mouthful."

"Yeah, I know."

"You do have a problem. Okay, let's hear it all. What were you in there for?"

Rick knew he couldn't hesitate. If he did it would sound like he was lying. "Throwing rocks at a stop sign," he answered.

Lon pulled on his beard. "That's it?"

"Well, it was lots of rocks, I guess. I didn't know when to quit."

"How long was your sentence?"

"Six months—that's the minimum there."

The biologist shook his head in disbelief. "Did you have priors? This wasn't your first offense?"

"Second. I stole a couple of CDs."

"Oh, now we're getting somewhere," Lon said sarcastically. With a snort he added, "Big-time bad guy you are."

"Really, I'm not lying."

Lon looked at him sharply, raised his voice. "You think I don't know these things happen?"

Rick was surprised by the man's reaction, by the anger in his voice. "Can I stay here until Josh comes back?"

"Of course you can. I don't know if I'm going to be able to do more for you than buy you a little time. . . . I have to start thinking about it."

Rick was shaking his head. "I'm not asking you to."

"I know you're not. What happens to you matters

to me, Rick. That's the way it is. Let's head down to camp. We can talk more there. And thanks for your help with the bird—you were terrific. I couldn't have done it without you."

15

It wasn't so easy to talk, to know where to begin. They ate, and then they sat on their lawn chairs and watched clouds boil enormously tall in the turquoise sky. "Can you fly in a cloud like that?" Rick asked.

"Oh, no," Lon replied. "Too much lift, too much turbulence, and of course you can't tell up from down. You get sucked up into one of those clouds, you'd probably tuck and tumble."

"What's that?"

"The nose would suddenly tuck under and you'd fall on the sail. The wing would be *underneath* you and spinning out of control. Even if you didn't tuck and tumble, the winds inside that cloud could tear your glider to shreds. Fortunately there's plenty of milder thermals that aren't associated with clouds; they're totally invisible. Those are the up elevators that we're always searching for."

"What exactly is a thermal?"

"A column of rising warm air. Warm air rises, cool air sinks. You spiral up on the thermal—a thousand feet per minute sometimes—then fly out of the thermal once you're as high as you want to go. As you leave the thermal, at first you'll descend fast on the cool air spilling down around the thermal's edge. Hang glider pilots call it going over the falls. Great sensation."

"Then what?"

"Then you glide into much more stable air. You're losing altitude, about a foot for every ten or twelve feet you're moving forward, at a rate of maybe two hundred feet per minute. As you glide, you're searching for another thermal. When you find the next one you climb up, up, up—"

"How high can you get?"

"Sixteen thousand feet is my ceiling. If you don't have oxygen, it's time to get off the up elevator. You repeat the same process over and over again. If it's a great flying day, and you're really catching thermals, you can fly distances. My personal best was 175 miles, from Owens Valley, California way into Nevada. What a workout that was."

Lon quit talking. Rick had a lot to think about, to imagine, as they watched the clouds turn dark.

"We're in for a show," Lon said. "Tents are battened—let her rip!"

"When do we release Maverick?"

"In the morning. He knows he's back at home base. No point in keeping him incarcerated. It's going to be up to him."

"How did you first get into birds?"

Memory kindled a fond smile in the man's weathered features. "Actually it was in one of my foster homes, when I was about your age. My foster dad was a vet."

Rick was jolted by surprise. "*You* were a foster kid?"

"More than once. How about you? Did you have a lot of different families?"

"Five," Rick answered. "The year before they sent me to the group home, I had three in one year. Nothing was working out. How many did you have?"

"You got me beat—four. Like I said, one of my foster fathers was a vet, dogs and cats mostly, but he started rehabilitating raptors on the side. Hawks and eagles. His name was Ernie, Ernie Wilson. You know, I haven't talked about this stuff in a zillion years. Nobody I felt like talking to about it, I guess."

Rick nodded.

"I used to make up stories a lot," Lon continued. "Like for people sitting next to you on buses who expect conversation. Whenever anybody would start asking about my life story I'd make up a different name for myself, invent childhood homes, parents. . . . I'd always make it different just to keep it interesting. You ever do that?"

Rick smiled. "Sure, all the time, but more with other kids—like when I'd be first starting at a new school. I used to say my father was a ref for the NBA, or a race car mechanic. I think my favorite one was telling people he was the lead singer in a band. Now *that* can get you respect."

Both of them were laughing, but Rick noticed that they were both looking away at the darkening clouds, not into each other's eyes.

Lightning snapped to the south, above the cliffs, and thunder came rumbling.

"Lon Peregrino isn't my original name," Lon said. "My first one was McDermott, Kenny McDermott. I was born in Atlanta, Georgia. Don't know a single thing about my mother except that she was a teenager and she skipped out of the hospital without taking me along. My father's a blank. McDermott is the name of the couple from Atlanta who adopted me."

The sky was almost black now above the cliffs, and lightning was cracking more and more frequently. "Coming our way," Lon said. "Let's move under the tarp. What about you, Rick? Start from the beginning. We got time."

Lon really did want to know, Rick realized. Once he began talking he was surprised to find that the words came easily. "I was born in San Jose, California. My mother was only fifteen when I was born, just a year older than I am now. She wasn't married or anything—just a clueless kid, I guess. A year or two later she ran off on me, and on her mother too—my grandmother. Went to L.A. with a different guy—not my father, whoever he was. My grandmother's the one who raised me, up until I was ten. My mother never called, never wrote, ever. My grandmother used to cry about it a lot when I was little."

"Could have been a lot worse," Lon said. "At least you had your grandma. It sounds like she was a nice lady, and I'll bet you were the apple of her eye."

Rick had to smile. He was picturing how proud his grandmother always was of him. "Sure, she used to brag about me to anyone who would listen. How about you? Did those McDermotts who adopted you have other kids?"

"No, it was just me, and I was always in the middle of their big fights. It was a pretty bad scene. They both drank, he kept losing jobs, things kept going from bad to worse. Then we up and moved to Boise, Idaho, when I was nine. They thought they'd start over in a new place; you know the dream. Well, it just got worse, the fighting and all. My mother moved back to Atlanta, left me with my dad. That's when he started beating up on me."

Rick was thinking about the kids in Blue Canyon, about Killian in particular.

"A teacher at school eventually figured out how bad it was," Lon continued. "The courts took me away from him, put me in foster care."

"With the vet and his family?"

"Actually, there were three different families before that. I guess I was really hard for them, a real angry kid. Then the vet and his family took me. Great people, really great people. That was my lucky day, the day I hooked up with Ernie."

It was starting to rain. Huge drops splattered the slickrock around them and the tarp drummed with liquid bullets. A lightning bolt lit up the camp like a photo flash, and thunder boomed like an explosion.

"Are we okay out here?" Rick asked, motioning toward the last big lightning bolt. The rain was turning to hail, rattling the tarp above them and pelting the wall tents.

"You got another location in mind?" Lon kidded him. "We're fine here, really. I love wild weather— don't you? Makes you feel alive!"

Rick was amazed at how easy it was talking to Lon. It didn't feel strange at all, and yet he'd never talked like this with anyone. He didn't want it to be over. "So you've been interested in birds ever since? Ever since the vet?"

The hail had turned to rain again. It was raining harder than Rick had ever seen. It was pouring off the tarp almost in a solid curtain. Lon had to raise his voice to be heard over the din.

"Let me tell you exactly how it happened," he said, moving closer so he didn't have to shout. "Not long after I moved in with Ernie's family, I found a bald eagle in a trap. I was hiking around, exploring behind their place—they lived a few miles out of McCall, Idaho—and I came across an eagle with its leg caught in one of those steel traps people set out for bobcats. We got it out of the trap, but it was hurt pretty bad. Ernie treated the eagle for blood poisoning. I took care of it every day, and we were able to release it forty-three days later. That was the happiest day of my life—seeing that bird fly away. Ernie could see I was fascinated, got me into learning more about eagles. His wife, my foster mom, was a librarian. She'd bring home books on birds, all different kinds. Well, you know how it all turned out. . . ."

They heard a rushing sound, the sound of cascading water. They jumped up to see if it might be a threat. The sound was coming from waterfalls, half a dozen of them, pouring brick red over the edge of the cliffs high above.

"Think what it's like down in the Maze right now," Rick said.

"Carving it all deeper. Now let's get back to you. I'm trying to picture you at the age of ten, when you lost your grandmother. What happened to her?"

"She got sick. It started when I was in about second grade, up in Fort Bragg, and just kept getting worse. For a long time I didn't know how serious it was. She'd go to the hospital for treatments, but she'd tell me not to worry. A lot of times there was nobody at home. I even started thinking it was kind of a good deal for me—I could just run around, do what I wanted. But then some neighbors turned me in, said I had no supervision at home, and the court put me in a foster home. My grandmother died a few months later."

The rain quit as abruptly as it had begun. The pouring of the waterfalls and the sound of the water rushing in the arroyos nearby continued. "I can sure remember what that's like," Lon said, "getting sent to those foster homes, shuffled around all the time. You hear stories about kids getting lucky, finding a good home right away and getting to stay there. I remember thinking it must be my fault."

Rick's head was nodding. "I know, I know."

"Just this last year I read an article about it. It said that after the age of ten, a kid's chances of getting adopted take a huge nosedive."

"A social worker told me that once. Sorta helped, but not really."

They stepped outside. The storm cell that had hammered them was attacking the Island in the Sky across the Green River with lightning bolt after lightning bolt. "Let's walk to the edge of the Maze," Rick suggested. "See what it looks like with water running in it."

They ran so they wouldn't miss the spectacle. When they got there, every pour-off along the rim was spilling torrents into the canyon. "Look at all those waterfalls!" Rick shouted.

The bottom of the canyon, normally bone dry, was

flooded with surging red waters. They found perches on a boulder next to a gnarled juniper where they could see below. Rick was eager to renew their conversation, not let it die out under the roar from the depths.

"When I first got here," he spoke up, "you asked if I had a stepfather who did this." He put a fingertip to the new scar over his cheekbone. "Is that how you got yours?"

"Yep," Lon replied.

"I'll bet you still hate him for that," Rick said with conviction.

Lon looked down into the canyon at the floodwaters. It was a long time before he spoke. "I used to have a chip on my shoulder about forty miles wide," he said finally. "I thought everyone had it in for me, and that the world was nothing but closed doors."

"It is."

"Those doors are in your outlook."

"What—Blue Canyon isn't real?"

"Sure it's real. But you have to play the hand you're dealt, Rick. You aren't the first kid who's ever been wronged, you know. Take a number, get in line."

Rick felt like he'd been stung. Why was Lon doing this when they'd been getting along so well? "Some things shouldn't be forgiven and forgotten," he insisted.

"Sounds like you're big on that. Nuke Carlile would agree with you, I'd bet. You have to move forward, wherever you are. Even if you wind up back at Blue Canyon—you have to move forward."

"What are you saying?"

"I'm saying it's time to move on, find your way into the clear, where you can shape your own life. I think you're getting mired down in your own personal tar pits. You need to focus on where you want to go and how you're going to get there."

Lon was starting to look uncomfortable, almost embarrassed. "Look, I'm not one for giving advice, Rick, but you're a special case. You're so much like who I was, it's scary."

It felt good hearing that, hearing there was a tie between them. "Find my way into the clear," Rick repeated wistfully. "That would be nice."

"Too much anger will eat you up from the inside— you'll spend your life looking backward. Keep just enough anger to stay honest, to keep your edge. Keep it for ballast. The rest, dump it."

"And fly out of a tar pit. Easier said than done."

"Well, I didn't say it would be easy, but I do know you have to do it."

"How? How do I do that?"

"You already know. You said the word just a few minutes ago. You gotta be willing to *forgive*. Can't move on until you do. I've learned that the hard way."

Rick was recalling something Mr. B. had said. Something about his break coming along one day and being ready to recognize it for what it was. Maybe meeting Lon was his break. "I'll think about it," he said.

"You got more kindness in you than I had, by a mile. Your grandmother taught you kindness. I was a little short on that score."

"So, how'd you get the name Lon Peregrino?" Rick asked. "You didn't tell me that part."

"Gave it to myself, after I got out of high school. I didn't go to college right away. I wanted to take some time and just explore the country, see some new places. I spent a couple years working ski patrol in the winters, doing a little construction in the summers, mostly grabbing every minute I could find to explore all these canyons in the Southwest."

Suddenly Rick was seeing handholds on the unclimbable mountain. "I can picture doing that."

"On one of my hikes I ran into some people working out in a camp like ours here, only they were working with falcons. Before that I'd never been able to picture a way that birds could be my life, like I'd dreamed. All of a sudden I could see something I really wanted to do. Of course I had to go to college . . . got a degree in bird biology so people would hire me."

"And your name? What about that?"

"Well, once I was studying birds, I got to thinking that my name should reflect more of who I was. I had never felt much like a McDermott, and Kenny didn't seem like a great fit either. So I came up with my own name—named myself after the falcons. They were peregrine falcons."

"Peregrine, Peregrino." Rick grinned. "Never thought of it till you said it. Does *peregrine* mean anything—I mean, besides being the name of the bird?"

"Traveler. It means traveler. Basically it refers to the distances they fly. They migrate to Mexico and Central America for the winter. The Lon part, I just liked it."

Lon got up, stretched, then pointed at the chest-high gnarled juniper next to him, growing out of a crack in the slickrock. "See this tree, Rick? It might be two hundred, three hundred years old. Never had much of a chance to flourish because it was born on such a rough spot. We've got it a heck of a lot easier. Just like this old juniper here, we might have been born in a rough spot, but at a certain point we realize we can help ourselves. We can pick up and move to better ground."

"I like your way of looking at it," Rick said.

"We'll never turn out cookie cutter normal, my friend, but we've got character. We're survivors, like those condors. Tough as condors too!"

16

The door of Maverick's prison was open, but the condor hadn't realized it yet. When the others started flying, around 10:00 A.M., Maverick moved from the rear of the pen to the front, stretched his neck excitedly, opened his beak wide, and started wagging his tongue. After running back and forth along the fence a couple times, he realized that the wire door was open.

Beating his wings, the condor hopped and ran down the slickrock ramp outside the pen and made a short flight to a boulder that was perched on the very edge of the cliff. No more than a minute passed, with Maverick eyeing the condors soaring above, before he bent at the knees, spread his wings wide, and launched himself from the cliffs.

Rick and Lon ran around the side of the release

pen in order to see what the condor was going to do. Rick was hoping that he didn't make another beeline across open country toward the Colorado River.

He didn't.

Maverick rose with the air rushing up the face of the cliffs, flapped a couple of times, then began to soar higher and higher. Instead of flying toward the others, who were a quarter mile north along the cliffs, the condor kept rising, flying up and up in great spiraling circles that reminded Rick of Lon's flight with the bald eagle.

The condor had risen so fast that it was very small in the sky and getting smaller. Lon was shading his eyes and looking straight up. "Unbelievable," he whispered. "He's caught a thermal. Look at him go! I wasn't expecting this for another month or two."

"That's Maverick for you," Rick said proudly.

Lon was glassing the bird with the binoculars now. "He's a couple thousand feet up and climbing."

"Is he ever coming back?"

"We'll find out. Let's take cover."

Maverick not only came back, he fed with the other condors again. They were soon flushed from a carcass by a golden eagle, who was joined by a few ravens and another golden. The second golden, nearly blond around its head and shoulders, wouldn't tolerate the ravens or even the other eagle on the carcass. When the first golden tried to move back in, the second flashed its talons briefly, then both took to the air, the blond one closing the distance as they gained altitude. With all their dodging and dive-bombing, they looked like two fighter pilots having a dogfight.

Several hundred feet above the rim and out in front of the cliffs, the eagles suddenly locked talons and fell spinning down the cliff face and out of view. Rick could scarcely believe what he'd just seen. "Are they going to crash, or what?"

"Very unlikely. They'll pull out. They have eight hundred feet to play with."

"I'm getting sick and tired of the eagles," Rick muttered. "I mean, they can hunt! I wish they'd just clear out and leave the carrion to the condors."

The biologist had a good chuckle. "So, the condors are the good guys and the eagles are the bad guys! Tell that to Sky!"

With Maverick back on track, Rick and Lon drove down to camp. Lon worked on his notes, and Rick's thoughts turned to the Maze.

"I'm going into the Maze this afternoon," he announced, remembering not to ask for Lon's blessing.

Lon's eyes looked troubled, as if he regretted his previous position, but he said nothing.

Rick packed up some snacks and a water bottle, found a way down into the closest canyon and walked for hours among its twists and turns. He passed dozens of side canyons. Each time a side canyon came in, he marked his path with a cairn of stones, as Lon had suggested. Without them it was almost impossible to tell, when he looked back, which way he had come. Everything looked the same: the same sequences of color in the smooth layers of slickrock, identical-looking dry pour-offs, the innumerable arching caves high above that were tucked under the rimrock.

Several times, out of curiosity, he turned up a side canyon to see if he could find an exit. Each time he was stopped by tall pour-overs and sheer cliffs. There were very few ways out.

Just as he was about to turn around and head back,

he did a double take. On the slick sandstone wall barely ahead there were drawings of fantastic figures, done in ancient, muted earth tones. He blinked and stared at the painted humanoid shapes, larger than life. Almost all of them had antennalike headgear. One had a cottonwood tree growing out of one of its fingers, or was it a cloud? He wondered if there was an ancient ruin close by. Was this one of the places Carlile had been looting? What a travesty that he wasn't going to get caught!

Climbing out of the Maze close to twilight exactly where he had entered, Rick was pleased with himself. This was easy compared with his personal maze, which didn't seem to have a single exit. Any path he picked was going to lead him back into Blue Canyon. It was only a matter of time.

"Wish I had some champagne," Lon remarked as Rick walked back into camp.

"You're that happy to see me?" Rick joked.

"Maverick roosted with the others. I believe our boy's going to make it."

In the morning Rick counted four condors preening high in the draw under the Needle carcass. Grooming themselves and arranging their flight feathers, Lon explained. One bird flew at 9:30 A.M. over to the pinnacle. Rick guessed it would be Maverick flying first, and it was. Lon identified him with the radio.

Maverick perched on the pinnacle for ten or fifteen minutes. Then he flew. Maverick soared back and forth across the rim, catching the lift rushing up the cliff face, and then he found another thermal. The condor spiraled up and up until he was a speck, farther yet until he disappeared. "Must be off to Wyoming," Lon declared. "Born to fly!"

They watched the others make impressive flights along the rim, but they didn't thermal. It was just after noon, when Lon was nibbling his hot dogs, that Rick saw a big bird flying in from the north. With the scope he verified that it was their prize flier returning and not an eagle.

They both heard the motor at the same time and looked toward the dugway. Carlile's rusty Humvee was descending the switchbacks. "Not now," Lon groaned.

Both turned quickly back to Maverick and the other condors. A seventh large bird was suddenly in the air, sleeker than the rest and a little smaller. Rick watched as the golden eagle climbed and plummeted repeatedly. After pulling out of a steep dive, it would climb swiftly. Then it would fold its wings until it stalled, dive, pull out, and climb again, repeating the sequence.

Maverick appeared to be gliding in for a landing by the Double Juniper carcass when the eagle dived on him from above, like a missile. Maverick aborted his landing and flew out over the rim. The eagle gave chase and bumped the condor in midair. Maverick peeled off, dropped altitude, and flapped away.

The eagle attacked again. "Lon!" Rick yelled. Rick was watching with the binoculars; Lon stood up to watch with his naked eyes.

Rick was aware of the Humvee pulling into camp behind them, but he didn't turn to look.

This time the eagle locked up with the condor. With their wings backstroking wildly, they were spinning down, out of control in front of the cliffs and losing altitude fast. It looked to Rick like the eagle might have a grip on Maverick with its talons.

To his immense relief, the birds separated before they hit the ground. Maverick ended up flying away from the cliffs and toward camp. He couldn't have been more than fifty feet off the ground. Rick saw Lon glance behind them, and then he did too. Nuke Carlile was out of his truck and watching the birds with the pit bull at his side. Gunderson was coming around the side of the Humvee for a better look. Both men had water jugs in hand.

"Get that dog back in your vehicle!" Lon yelled. "Now!"

Carlile did nothing. He stood stiff as a fencepost and continued to watch the birds.

"I said, get it in the truck!"

The pit bull was growling at Lon while its eyes remained fixed on the birds.

The eagle, having gained altitude again, stooped once more, straight down on the condor, and this time forced Maverick to the ground. In a frenzy of beating wings, the birds were locked together out on the open ground no more than two hundred feet away. Rick saw the flash of the eagle's talons.

Lon hollered at the top of his lungs, as if the sound of his voice might drive the birds apart. It didn't, and Lon took off sprinting. "Bring the net, Rick!" he screamed over his shoulder.

Carlile might have whispered a command. Suddenly the dog's claws were scratching for traction on the slickrock as it charged explosively in pursuit of the birds.

It took a few seconds for Rick to get to the net in the back of the truck. By the time he turned himself around and started running back toward Lon, the eagle was in the air and climbing. Maverick, beating his tired wings as hard as he could, was in flight but only a few feet off the ground, with the pit bull closing in and Lon desperately trying to catch up.

"Climb, Maverick!" Rick screamed as he ran.

The condor was within an eyelash of escaping. With a last thrust of its hind legs, the pit bull leaped and caught the bird in its jaws, dragged it down, and began to maul it. A second later Lon threw himself on the back of the dog, stood up with the pit bull locked in a bear hug. Lon was cursing at the top of his lungs.

The dog kicked its legs and writhed its spine to try to get free of the man but still wouldn't let go of the bird. Lon leaned forward and bit the dog's ear as hard as he could. Enraged, the dog finally dropped the huge bird.

The condor fell in a heap to the ground. Rick saw the dog's jaws turn on the man. Lon thrust the dog away from himself and pursued it with a kick that failed to connect. In a moment the pit bull would have had Lon's leg in its jaws. Rick raised the net high and slammed it to the ground over the dog.

The pit bull went insane with fury, snarling and gnashing at the net and trying to rise. Lon had Maverick in his arms and was carrying him toward the camp kitchen.

Rick stood on the net's handle as close as he dared, in order to keep the dog pinned down.

"Let go that dog!" he heard Carlile rasp behind him.

"You think I'm crazy?" Rick demanded.

The second man dropped his plastic jug, lumbered up, and barreled Rick off his feet. Rick fell backward looking into a face contorted with hate. The pit bull lunged at him from the side, but he saw it coming and

managed to roll. The dog caught only the hem of his
jeans leg.

"Hold, Jasper, hold!" came Carlile's hoarse command. Baring its fangs, snarling, the dog wasn't going
to quit. Carlile reached for its collar.

Rick regained his feet and started backing away.

"You," the man said, his face livid with spidery red
blood vessels. "I've seen you before. At my station."

"It's a small world," Rick said bitterly.

"You his son?"

"Nephew."

"The bird's dead, Carlile," Lon called.

"It was an accident," the man snarled back. "Just
came to get water."

"Fill them and get out."

There was a smirk on Gunderson's fleshy face.
"Mess with us . . ." he said to Rick. "For crying out
loud, it's only a vulture!"

Carlile made his dog get in the Humvee. The two
men ambled with their water containers toward the
spring.

Rick despised them for lingering after what they'd
done. He wanted to hurt them, and hurt them bad,
though he couldn't see a way. Still short of breath from
his battle with the dog, he went to join Lon, who was
standing under the kitchen tarp next to the body of
the condor.

Maverick was splayed on top of the kitchen table.
The condor was a heap of torn flesh and broken feathers. Nature's most magnificent flying machine, Rick
thought bitterly. Maverick's eyes were glazed and dry,
and his tongue stuck out grotesquely.

"Too far, too fast," Lon whispered.

Rick couldn't help himself. Tears were streaming

down his face. He realized he was sobbing out loud. He'd never forget what it was like holding that ancient bird in the front seat of the truck, what its beating heart had felt like under his hand.

Lon stepped aside as Rick put his hand to the lifeless bird's breast. It was still warm.

Lon's eyes were brimming, his voice breaking. "Too close to the sun, Maverick. You flew too close to the sun."

Like Icarus, Rick realized.

"He was quite a bird," the man said softly. "Such a superb, beautiful bird. He was carrying some of the best flying genes in his species' extremely limited gene pool."

Rick had nothing to say. He backed slowly away from the table and turned to shield his tears. All the hopelessness in his life seemed to be welling up and spilling over. Life really *was* unfair, rank with malice and viciousness.

Rick wiped his eyes. As they cleared, he noticed the two men over at the spring. He focused all his anger and all his hate on them. He only wished there was a way to avenge the condor on them.

When he had himself under control he turned back to Lon. The biologist's old scar glistened wet and shiny. Lon plucked one of the long primary feathers from the dead bird's wing tip. It was easily twenty inches long. "For you," he said.

The feather was light as air in Rick's fingers. "Do we bury him?" he asked weakly.

"We put him on ice; there'll have to be an autopsy. I'm going to radio the park in a few minutes—arrange to talk directly with Josh tonight. There's a place he can drive to about an hour out of Vermilion Cliffs where his signal's got a good shot at the repeater on the Island in the Sky."

Rick was still so numb he barely heard what Lon was saying. An autopsy sounded so scientific and so pointless.

The pair from Hanksville was headed back from the spring. Carlile walked with his head up and shoulders back, as ever. Gunderson lumbered aggressively forward with shoulders hunched and one arm akimbo. "Don't say a word," Lon whispered.

The two passed silently through camp. They paused long enough to glare contemptuously at the biologist and the dead bird.

Rick watched the Humvee drive away to the east, toward the Standing Rocks. He went into his tent to get away. It wasn't easy to accept Lon's helplessness and his own.

He heard the biologist enter his own tent.

Ten minutes later Lon appeared at the door of Rick's. "There's only one way I can deal with this," the man said. "By flying."

There was a question in Lon's eyes, and Rick had a good guess what it was.

"Now, you can say no . . . but do you want to fly tandem with me? A Maverick Memorial Flight?"

"I say yes."

17

The glider was rigged and they were done with the rehearsals. They were harnessed, helmeted, hooked in and waiting.

Rick watched the green streamer at the cliff edge. As soon as it blew strong directly toward them, it would be time to go. He was afraid in every nerve but his adrenaline was pumping and he was full of resolve. He knew exactly why he wanted to do this. It might be for Maverick, but it was also for him.

"What do you think, Rick? We can do some ridge soaring along the cliffs here and then head out onto the flats for a landing, or we can stay up awhile longer and do some thermaling. If I find a thermal, that is."

"What's that going to be like?" Rick asked tentatively.

"It'll feel like you're going up the express elevator.

If we do that, we can really sky out over the desert, but I have to warn you there'll be some rock 'em, sock 'em on the way. There's always some amount of turbulence in a thermal."

"We'd catch one thermal and then come down?"

"All depends on you. We could fly out of one thermal and glide until we catch another one. But don't worry, I'm not planning on breaking any distance records on your first flight."

Rick gathered his courage. "This is the Maverick Memorial Flight. Let's go for a thermal."

"Had a hunch you'd say that. Hope I can find one for you."

"Promise me none of those clouds are going to suck us up. I don't want to find out what it's like to tuck and tumble."

"Those aren't monster clouds, and we'll stay away from them. If we don't catch a thermal, we won't even make it to the primary LZ. We'll use that big patch of red dirt you see over there by Chimney Rock, a couple hundred yards from where those guys pitched camp."

"I see it. Close to the edge of the Maze."

"If we get into a thermal and you don't like the feeling—if it spooks you bad or you feel like you're getting airsick—just point your thumb at the ground. We'll break out and soar for home. Hey, look at our wind streamer. Changing direction."

It was time. It was all a matter of faith in Lon Peregrino, the man at his side who'd named himself after a bird.

I've only known him for seven days, Rick reminded himself.

That doesn't matter. I trust him.

Rick looked down the gentle ramp of slickrock to

the edge of the sky, so close at hand. He breathed deep, tried to calm his heart. Only thirty feet separated him from his leap of faith. Lon had done all his safety checks. Their harnesses were attached to separate locking carabiners suspended from the keel overhead.

"Still waiting," Lon said, intent on the green strip. "Most of flying is *waiting* to fly."

Then Lon asked with a grin, "Anything on your mind? Any last questions?"

"That song you sing . . . I've been thinking a lot about those 'Buffalo Gals.'"

"You have?"

"I mean, are they girls or are they female buffaloes?"

"Strange . . . I think about that too. Can't give you the answer, though."

"Too bad."

"It's like life—long on questions and short on answers."

"I guess I do have a question. I don't have a parachute on the pouch over my chest here."

"Mine would do for us both. Don't worry, I've never deployed one. But you're right, you should know what would happen. It's not possible to disconnect ourselves from the glider. I'd take the parachute out and throw it clear."

"The ship would go down with us?"

"That's right. Sounds messy, but it works. Now put that out of your mind. I'm going to give you a glory ride, not a ride to glory. All set?"

"I'm set."

"Remember what I told you. Don't touch that control bar. Let me do the flying." Lon wrapped his arms around the outside of the downtubes and hefted the glider off the ground. "Ready?"

Rick took another deep breath. "Ready!"

"*Clear*! One, two, three, *Go*!"

Rick focused on staying in step. At the halfway mark, he picked up the pace as planned. The edge of the cliff seemed to rush forward to meet him.

He didn't hold back. This was his dream.

Even before the edge Rick felt a sudden hoist, and his feet left the ground. Then came the impact of the air rushing up the cliff face and the powerful lift of the wing. He reached with his left arm around Lon's back and hung on to his side.

As soon as Lon brought his hands from the downtubes to the control bar in front of him and below, Rick hung on to the pilot's upper right arm with his free hand. With a glance down, Rick's vision swam—the world had fallen out below. His stomach went into free fall. The thought raced through him like an electrical discharge: *This is not going to be okay.*

Panicky, he was about to reach forward for the control bar; it was right down there in front of him. But Lon had warned him. If he grabbed hold of the control bar they were going to be in big trouble in a big hurry. Flying the glider was a delicate matter and the pilot didn't need any help.

Don't look down, Rick reminded himself. He was trying to kick into the bottom of his harness cocoon with his right foot, but he couldn't find it. He wasn't going to be able to hang horizontally until he did. "Take your time, Rick," the pilot said coolly. "No rush. We're doing fine."

In fact, they were already several hundred feet away from the cliff, level and steady. Rick felt a surge of confidence that everything was okay, that he hadn't somehow wrecked the takeoff. He was flying!

At last his right foot found the inside of the bag, and his left foot followed. With his right hand he pulled on the cord that controlled the bag's zipper, then resumed his grip on Lon's arm. He was all zipped up and perfectly prone, the way he was supposed to be.

Now that he was properly positioned in his cocoon, suspended alongside Lon and helmet to helmet, he could give himself over to the exhilaration. He was flying. Actually flying!

Rick allowed himself to look down. They were passing directly over the camp, a thousand feet above it and rising. The instrument on Lon's control bar— the variometer—showed their elevation at 6,200 feet above sea level. The chirp tone meant they were rising.

Lon pushed the control bar away from himself; Rick felt the lift as they rose higher. Shifting his body weight, and consequently Rick's, Lon executed a gradual turn. Soon they were soaring along the line of the red cliffs but high above them.

Lon circled back until they were high over the spot where they'd launched. As they turned north once more, the pilot freed his right hand from the control bar and pointed below. "What do you see?"

Now Rick saw them, all soaring. "Five condors!"

"Let's go find that thermal!"

Lon steered away from the cliffs and out toward the Standing Rocks. Rick knew Lon wasn't finding his column of rising air—the variometer was buzzing, which meant they were losing altitude. Rick could see the secondary landing zone ahead: the red dirt patch near Chimney Rock, not far from Carlile's blue tarp.

He started thinking about the landing. Unless Lon found rising air soon, this was going to be a short flight. Let Lon stall the glider and put his feet on the ground before you touch down, he reminded himself.

Then it happened. Directly over Lizard Rock they entered a thermal. There was no doubt about it. The glider was rocked suddenly, and Rick felt the terrific lift. "Up we go!" Lon shouted. He was making adjustments with his hands to swing their combined body mass to the right or the left.

They were into turbulence—major turbulence, it seemed to Rick—and taking a terrific buffeting. It's not that bad, Rick reassured himself. With a glance down he could see the earth falling away at an incredible rate. The variometer kept chirping as Lon negotiated his spirals.

Skyward they rose on that great thermal upcurrent, thousands of feet higher. He thought of Maverick, what this must have felt like for Maverick on his two thermal rides just yesterday and this morning. To feel the air under his wide wings lifting him up and up, to discover that this was what he was born for . . .

With a glance down Rick saw the Maze laid out below, all its intricate, twisting, convoluted canyons draining toward the Green River. It was all so easy to read from the air, as he'd imagined it would be—nothing like being down in it.

"Fourteen thousand feet," Lon announced a few minutes later. "Let's call it good—getting marginal without oxygen!"

Lon steered out of the turbulence, and then they took a sudden drop that felt like a stomach plunge on a roller coaster. "Over the falls!" Lon called.

Rick's stomach was going to be okay. Lon glided into smooth air and they hovered over the Green River, over the Island in the Sky, over the confluence of the Green and the Colorado. Rick could see a thousand canyons and more, all at once.

At eight thousand feet Lon caught another thermal, and they skyed out over the desert again, rising all the way up to 14,463 feet. They soared over the confluence of the rivers again, over the Island in the Sky, back across the Green, over the Maze.

When the time came to return to earth, Lon made it look so easy. They glided in over the formations of the Doll House. Lon circled his landing zone once, then turned into the wind. They hit the ground running.

It wasn't until the condors had roosted and the cliffs were lit by the moon that the return to Lon's call came crackling over the radio. "How's everything in the Maze?" asked Josh's cheerful voice.

Lon told of Maverick's death without ever using the condor's name. He only called him M4. Lon's account was dispassionate, scientific. Rick kept waiting for him to explain that this had been no accident, that Carlile had loosed the dog on purpose.

"Tough loss," came the voice from the Vermilion Cliffs.

"Tough, tough loss," Lon agreed.

What Lon said next took Rick completely by surprise. "Josh, I want you to get set to relieve me here when you drive in the evening of the fifteenth. Plan for a two-week cycle. Maybe you and Andrea both, if David can hold the fort there. I have some personal business I have to attend to."

There was a moment's hesitation from the other end. "Anything I can help with? Is anything wrong?"

"I'll tell you all about it when you come in. Ice a cooler especially for M4."

As Lon signed off, Rick couldn't contain his frustration any longer. "You didn't tell him how it really happened!"

"Carlile's camp is just a few miles down the road, and he's got a radio. He might have been listening in. I expect this is his last trip to take out his contraband—there's no point in getting him stirred up. I'll tell Josh an earful when he gets here."

"What's this about you leaving? What's that all about?"

Lon shrugged. "It's about you. I'm going to drive you out. I've been thinking it over all day."

"Drive me where?"

"All the way to Reno. Try to get a hearing with the judge who sent you to Blue Canyon. I intend to stand up for you."

Rick didn't know what to say. He would never have guessed that Lon would leave his condors. "You don't have to do that," he mumbled. Here was a glimpse of hope.

"'Course I don't," Lon said gruffly. "Don't know if I can do you any good either, but I want to try. I have a question for you. It seems to me you could use another ally. Got any suggestions? Anybody else who might speak for you in front of that judge?"

"The librarian at Blue Canyon. His name's Mr. B."

18

Rick lay on the cot feeling weightless. All he had to do to recapture the sensation of flight was to close his eyes.

It was the greatest feeling in the world. The only way to improve upon it would be to control the glider himself. He could imagine what that would feel like, having his hands on the control bar and soaring, making turns, looking way down at the revolving earth.

As he fell asleep, his conscious images melded seamlessly into dream images. He had a new kind of flying dream, not the miraculous hovering. This time his hands were on the control bar of a brightly colored artificial wing. He was shifting his body weight, actually controlling the glider as he spiraled up and up, then soared over the shifting shapes of the canyon-lands. Climb and glide, climb and glide, all night long. If it went on forever, that would be fine by him.

In the morning everything looked a little different. In the aftermath of flying with Lon, nothing seemed impossible. Surviving Blue Canyon, even that seemed possible.

Lon's eyes made contact over the rim of his coffee cup. He took a drink and set the cup down. Blue Canyon turned out to be on his mind too. "Don't expect any miracles," Lon said. "I think it's likely a question of keeping your next sentence down to the minimum."

"Believe me, I'm not expecting miracles—I remember that judge. He disliked me in particular."

"So let's not talk about it for now. Let's talk about hang gliding. Do you think you might want to pilot a hang glider someday?"

"I know I do."

"How come?"

"How come? Same reason as you—I want to fly! Now that I've done it, I can't stop thinking about it."

"You know you have to be strong to fly, to handle that control bar, wrestle the big wing. How many pull-ups can you do?"

"I was doing eighteen consistently at Blue Canyon."

"That's got me beat. Takes a cool head too, good nerves, but I think you've got that covered. Now I get to feel responsible for getting you into this, whatever happens." A grin was spreading across Lon's face. "'Course it's not like your parents will sue me."

They both laughed, but Rick's was nervous laughter. "You aren't talking about now . . . about teaching me to fly *now*, are you?"

"No time like the present. It'd take us fifteen minutes to get ready to go."

The idea thrilled him and terrified him at the same time. "You can't mean really flying by myself? Is there a bunny hill around here or something? No way I'm going to jump off a cliff."

"There's a perfect place to catch just a little air— the dunes right above the LZ. I'll grab the portable radio. It'll give you a leg up if I coach you through the receiver in your helmet. The condors don't get active until late morning; we'll be back in camp by then. Let's go!"

It took them closer to thirty minutes to get ready. Lon couldn't find the fold-up antenna for the portable two-way radio even though he went through everything in his tent twice looking for it. "I remember setting it on my footlocker last night," he said. "I'm positive—that's where I always keep it. Oh, well, I can use the one in the truck if I stand real close."

The pickup jolted through the potholes as they neared Carlile's camp at Chimney Rock—a wall tent and a tarp, a couple of card tables. Rick tensed. There was no way to avoid passing close by. Carlile was pouring coffee. His partner was flipping pancakes. The two stared. The dog barked.

Rick stared back at them. "How come this time they set up camp?" he wondered aloud. "Think it means they're staying awhile?"

"I don't even want to guess," Lon replied irritably as the truck began to descend the ridge into the sandy gullies that led to the landing zone and the dunes.

Rick decided to change the subject. He had something he'd been wanting to ask. "When Maverick died, you said something about flying too close to the sun. Isn't that what happened to Icarus, in the story from Greek mythology?"

"You know about Icarus! I love that story. But I have this theory, Rick. . . . I never bought the bit about the sun melting the wax that held the wings together. Everybody knows that as you go higher up in the atmosphere, it gets colder, not warmer."

"It's just a story, Lon."

"What if it *wasn't*? The Greeks were about the smartest people who ever lived, and Daedalus was the most brilliant inventor who ever lived. His time might have been thousands of years ago, but let's give him the credit he's due. Suppose for a minute that the Icarus story is a poetic account of something that *actually happened*."

"That would be amazing."

"Imagine for a moment that Daedalus actually built two devices, very much like modern hang gliders, one for himself and one for his son."

"I like this theory of yours."

"Here's what happened. Very simply, Icarus got caught in a thermal he wasn't experienced enough to handle. It took him up and up, who knows how many thousands of feet up—"

"And then he tucked and tumbled into the sea."

"That's it."

"Icarus flew out of a maze, you know."

The driver's grin was back. "Interesting. . . . Hey, wait a minute!"

Lon had stepped hard on the brake, and he was staring down at the base of the gearshift. He'd suddenly gone pale. "Radio's gone!"

Rifling through the assorted junk between them, Lon came up with the mike attached to its coil and jack, but no radio.

"Carlile?" Rick wondered.

"During the night, I guess. Must've stolen the antenna too, for the portable, right off my footlocker."

"Your truck antenna, Lon! Look, it's been snipped off!"

Lon stared at the spot, unbelieving. "We're out of communication, Rick. We've got the portable in my dresser, but it has no range without an antenna. He's cut us clean off."

A bolt of fear had every nerve in Rick's body buzzing. "Why?" he asked, trying to glimpse what was coming.

The biologist's features reflected the extreme frustration and anger that had been building inside. "I'm not scaring out of here. They're going to find out I'm not that easy to run off."

"I just remembered something," Rick said. He felt sick.

"Remembered what?"

"When Carlile was telling Gunderson about the stuff that was in your tent, he mentioned that you had a two-way radio in there. Maybe that's what he was trying to find out—if you had a second radio."

"Makes sense. He was threatened by my having the capability to report on his activities. Which I did, very shortly thereafter. This time he made sure I couldn't do it again. Hey, don't get mad at yourself."

Get even, Rick thought, but he didn't say it. He asked, "So you don't think he'll steal other stuff too?"

"Looks like it was the radios he was after. Let's just hope he takes the last of his contraband out on this trip—in that case we'll have seen the last of him. I can guarantee you the Condor Project won't be buying gas from him anymore, that's for sure. Let's forget about him, Rick. Get you started with the hang glider."

They parked on the side of the road next to the head of the landing zone. Lon tied a green wind streamer to the branch of a juniper, and then they trudged up and around the side of the dune field that sloped gently down to the landing zone from a cluster of sand hilltops. Rick was carrying the furled seventy-five-pound solo glider over his shoulder while Lon walked behind with the duffel bag. "Set it down and rest a spell," Lon called.

"I can't. I'm too psyched to rest. Are we going up to the top of those dunes up there?"

"Not today, not a chance." Lon led him out onto the center of the dune field, onto a sand bench a football field's length from the landing zone and no more than thirty feet above it.

Rick laid the long bundle down gently on the sand. As he looked down the slope, he realized it was time to focus. "I'm ready," he said quietly.

"That streamer is pretty limp down there. Not much wind; this isn't the top of the Condor Cliffs. We'll take our time assembling the glider. I'll tell you what everything is and what it's for. Theory is important. You can't control the glider without understanding the principles."

Rick watched with utter concentration as Lon began to assemble the glider. He focused on the order of each step as Lon slowly described what he was doing. Rick concentrated on the names of every member. He committed the theory to memory: air rushing over the wing has farther to travel than the air underneath. The difference makes lower pressure over the wing. Low pressure above the wing creates lift.

At last the wind was blowing and Rick was harnessed. He was helmeted and poised for his first attempt, wearing a long shirt of Lon's, a pair of jeans, and Lon's hard plastic knee pads. Sticking his head under the joint where the downtubes met the keel, he wrapped his arms around the tubes and lifted. The streamer he'd been watching suddenly went limp. He had to set the glider back down on its wheels.

Half a dozen times he lifted the glider in anticipation, only to have to set it down. Finally the wind held, and Lon gave the nod. *"Clear!"* Rick yelled. He began to walk, then to jog, then to run. Whatever happened, he wouldn't have very far to fall.

At the edge of the sand bench he felt the sensation of lift. He was about to be lifted from the ground, but something went wrong. His momentum took him over the edge, and the slope seemed to rush up to meet him. The glider crashed on its nose, and he was dragged on his face and chest through the sand.

"What happened?" he sputtered as Lon ran to help him up.

"Partly not enough airspeed, partly it was your angle of attack. We'll talk it over and try again."

He tried all morning. He spilled the glider on its nose and onto both sides, and he stalled it backward. The wind was good, and he'd been lifted time and again free of the ground, but he hadn't really flown. It was difficult knowing exactly when to move his hands down to the control bar. After he accomplished that, it was difficult to know what to do with his hands on the bar and when it needed to be done.

It was easy enough in theory. "When you push your body back relative to the bar, the glider climbs and decelerates," Lon had said. "When you push your body forward over the bar, the glider dives down and accelerates."

Theory and practice were two different things. It didn't seem to come naturally, knowing whether to pull himself over the bar or to push himself back from it. "Shift your grip—and consequently your body weight—to the right, you'll steer to the right. Shift your body weight to the left, you'll steer to the left."

He knew Lon wanted to get back to his birds. "One more try," Rick almost pleaded.

"You have quite an appetite for sand."

And then he flew! Miraculously, it seemed, he felt the lift as he approached the dune face, and he responded with the right moves at the right time. The sensation was unmistakable, a thrill beyond anything he'd expected. He was flying on his own, by himself! He flew two hundred yards straight down over the landing zone, ten, twenty feet above the ground.

True, he blew the landing. It wasn't that he didn't land into the wind; the wind remained blowing against him as it should. He forgot to reach up for the downtubes early enough, to stall the glider as he'd been taught, in order to land on his feet like a parachutist touching down.

He ended up flopping on his belly and his knees. It didn't matter, he'd been doing that all morning. He was okay, and he had flown, actually flown. He let out a victory whoop as Lon came running across the field.

"What an inaugural flight! Took me two or three days to pull that off when I was learning."

"It felt good. Unbelievably good. I want more!"

"Tomorrow."

19

On their way back to the condors, the road forced them once again to pass by the edge of Carlile's camp at the base of Chimney Rock. The tent and the tarp were still in place, but the Humvee was gone and there was no sign of life. Without a word being spoken, Rick knew the biologist too was seeing the death of his magnificent Maverick over and over in his head. "What about your radio and the antennas?" Rick suggested. "Should we search their camp?"

"I think not," Lon replied measuredly. "Let's not play games with these guys."

Back in his own camp Lon wolfed his customary hot dogs, reached for his binoculars, and began to scan the rim high above. It was apparent he intended to block all thoughts of Carlile and Gunderson, what they must be doing at this moment, since he was powerless to do anything about it. "Heading out in a minute to take some more bird feed up top," Lon said with forced cheerfulness. "I'm looking forward to spending the afternoon observing the five."

Rick's feelings must have shown. He wasn't ready to look at the rest of the birds, not yet.

"You can just hang out," Lon suggested. "Take a nap."

Rick nodded his agreement.

"Put the spotting scope away if it rains."

It might never have happened if Lon hadn't mentioned the spotting scope. As soon as Lon drove out, the high-powered telescope mounted on the tripod became a temptation that grew more irresistible by the moment. How easy it would be to throw it in a daypack and take off on the bike. From the top of Lizard Rock, with that scope, he would be able see a long, long way. Maybe he could see something, at no risk to himself, that would eventually turn the tables on the pothunters.

At the base of Lizard Rock he hid the mountain bike behind a juniper and began climbing. Once he reached the nearly level top of the immense mound of stone, more than a hundred feet above the ground, he kept on his belly and inched forward until the view opened to the east and north.

He could see Carlile's camp, still empty, and he could see the canyons of the Maze writhing like snakes north toward the Green River. All but one twisted and turned upon themselves; one ran north in virtually a straight line. He spread out the map he'd taken from the bookcase in his tent, located Lizard Rock, oriented the map by using the Island in the Sky. The straight-running canyon was Jasper, the one

Nuke had named his dog after. The one the park had closed.

A canyon that was off limits, he realized, would be the safest possible place for pothunters to hide their plunder.

Jasper Canyon's southernmost fingers reached within half a mile of Carlile's camp at Chimney Rock. Nuke must have camped there for a reason.

It all fit together. Carlile's cache of artifacts was located somewhere in Jasper Canyon's ten-mile run to the Green River.

Rick scanned Jasper's rims with the spotting scope. As far as he could see, the slickrock rims above Jasper Canyon looked like they might be accessible to a Humvee. But he couldn't spot the Humvee.

He had to get closer, and he had an idea how to do it—through the Maze. On his map he could see a trail leading out of a side canyon west of Jasper. It led onto a ridge overlooking Jasper Canyon.

Stealthily he worked his way down the flanks of Lizard Rock, then slipped into the Maze down a side finger of the canyon he'd identified from the map and from observation.

Every few hundred yards another canyon would come in from one side or the other, sometimes both sides at once. He concentrated hard, trying to commit them to memory. As he continued cautiously down the dry creekbed, the hair stood up on the back of his neck. Thunder was rumbling far away, and it made him even more uncomfortable. He knew he'd come a couple of miles. He'd seen the effect of water rushing in these canyons. It was time to find the trail that was on the map or backtrack for home. He decided to give it five more minutes.

He found the trail. Halfway up it he came upon a stairway of crude stone blocks that had been built to cross a pitch of steep slickrock. One of Carlile's cattle stairways, he realized, from decades before.

As the trail cleared the cleft it had followed through the rimrock, he duckwalked and then bellied onto the crest of the ridge. Suddenly he was looking down into the depths of Jasper Canyon.

Jasper was a sheer-walled jewel. He took the spotting scope out of his daypack and scanned the rims in both directions, as far as he could see. Nothing.

The sky was darkening and the wind was beginning to blow. It was time to give this up.

He was about to put the scope away when movement caught his eye. Something was moving in one of three arching caves across the canyon, several hundred yards to the south. The movement was behind a line of bushes that grew along the front edge of the cave, where the water dripping from the rim had allowed them to take root.

Through a slight gap in the bushes he detected a man. A man on one knee was making some sort of repetitive motion with his arms. Rick held the scope as still as he could, brought the man into focus. It was the big man. It was Gunderson. He was filling a military-green metal box with objects he was transferring from a larger box.

What were those things? Rick adjusted the focus delicately. They were cylindrical, metallic-looking, about eight inches long and three or so inches in diameter, with caps on both ends. Gunderson was very carefully placing them, one after the other, into the box.

Whatever they were, they weren't ancient pottery.

From Rick's vantage point, at this time of day, the west-facing cave was lit extremely well, and he was glad for it. He nudged the scope off Gunderson, paused at another gap in the brush. His breath caught short. Against the rear wall of the cave, five military-style rifles with large ammunition clips were propped next to a weapon with a wide tube for a barrel. A rocket launcher? A grenade launcher? What were the rifles—assault rifles?

He swiveled the scope back to Gunderson's cylinders.

Pipe bombs? Was that possible?

Gunderson snapped down the lid of the metal box he'd been loading, then lifted it and walked to the corner of the cave. How had he gotten into that cave? It looked impossible. Sheer cliff adjoined the cave walls on both sides.

Then Rick caught sight of the answer. A thick board had been placed across the gap between the cave and a nearby ledge. Without the plank the cave was accessible only to birds.

He'd seen too much, he realized—enough to cost him his life. These men were much more dangerous than he or Lon had ever guessed. Anyone who would manufacture a bomb . . .

The weather was threatening, but he knew better than to try to get back to camp along the rim. He'd be totally exposed. Keeping low, he turned around and slipped back down into the Maze the same way he had come.

He was more concerned about the weather now, and he was moving as fast as he could. The lightning and thunder were getting closer all the time, and the wind was beginning to blow hard.

Suddenly all the canyons looked the same. Earlier he hadn't taken the time to pile up rock cairns to mark the way back. He'd hadn't figured to return this way. Frantically he searched for footprints, found none. It was all slickrock.

Rick stopped at the confluence of two identical-looking canyons. He had to choose. He chose the one at his left.

Ten minutes later he knew he hadn't come this way before. Yet it looked like a way out, and with the storm about to break he had to take it.

At last he was looking at the final climb. He thought there was a route he could piece together up among the ledges that would lead him to a diagonal seam in the topmost layer, the rimrock.

And it worked. Hand over hand, he pulled himself onto the rim. Heaving for breath, he discovered he'd emerged much closer to Chimney Rock than Lizard Rock. He was nowhere near his bike. He was too close to the head of Jasper Canyon, too close to the route Carlile and Gunderson would use between their cache and camp.

He took off jogging, but he didn't have the breath. After a minute he had to stop. Bent over double, he gasped for breath.

Rick heard a bark and then an insane-sounding burst of alarms from the throat of the dog. Over his shoulder he saw the Humvee heading for the camp at Chimney Rock, trying to beat the rain. The dog had been running alongside, but now it was running toward him.

He ran west toward Lon's camp, but camp was several miles away. He was running as fast as he possibly could, but he was running directly into the wind. With a glance over his shoulder he saw the dog coming hard; it had closed the gap by half and now was only a hundred yards behind. The Humvee had veered in his direction too, but it was rumbling laboriously over terrain that looked like it should be impassable.

There just wasn't any choice. He could outrun the Humvee but not the dog. He ran down a slickrock incline into a canyon finger shaped like a racing speedway banked on both sides. The rust-colored dog, barking maniacally, was close behind.

Before long the walls were a hundred feet high and narrowing. It felt like he was running down an alley between high buildings. He had to hope for a pour-over, a jump that he could make but that the dog wouldn't. He just had to hope that it wasn't too much of a jump.

Another half minute and here it was, an eight-foot jump down to the next level. He took it, tumbling to reduce the impact on his knees.

He looked back up. There was the dog, panting, whining, barking, but stopped. Stopped.

Rick took off running. The narrow side canyon turned a bend fifty yards later. Very shortly he found himself decelerating, by degrees at first and then rapidly pulling up to a complete stop.

A few feet in front of him the canyon fell away into air, nothing but air. How could this have happened to him? Of all the bad luck! A few cautious steps forward, and he found himself standing at the lip of a sheer dropoff that left him fifty or sixty feet above the bottom of the canyon.

Lightning snapped suddenly and was followed only seconds later by thunder like a sonic boom. The sky had turned dark, extremely dark, and the wind was blowing a gale.

He ran back the way he had come, already doubtful that it was possible to climb the pour-over where he'd jumped. The dog was still up there, looking over its shoulder for the two men. When the pit bull saw him below, it resumed its insane alarms. Rick looked desperately for fingerholds, footholds. He could picture all too well the waterfall that was going to come pouring through here perhaps in a matter of minutes. There was no choice but to holler for help. "Carlile!" he yelled. "Nuke!"

As soon as he yelled the man's name he realized that Carlile was going to want to know where he'd been. He had to get rid of the spotting scope, just in case.

Rick ran around the bend in the box canyon, whipped the daypack off his back, removed the spotting scope, and set it down on the slickrock.

He put the daypack back on and raced around the corner. When he got back, Carlile and Gunderson were standing above the drop. The dog erupted again, but Carlile, with a command, shut it up.

"I need a hand up," Rick panted. "I'd sure appreciate it."

Gunderson was gloating. Carlile was much more focused. His thin lips were drawn tight, his gray eyes suspicious. "Where you been this afternoon?"

"Down in the Maze," Rick said truthfully. "Exploring the Maze."

"You're an idiot, then, with the weather coming on."

"That may be," Rick admitted. "It's all new to me. I didn't know any better."

"What's in your pack—that shape?"

"Water bottle."

"Toss the pack up."

Rick did, and Carlile removed the plastic water bottle, which was all but empty. He put it back inside, tossed the pack down. "Self-reliance is a virtue," Carlile said acidly. His partner was smirking as he studied the slick surface to the side of the cavity under the pour-over. It didn't look climbable.

Lightning cracked again, thunder exploded, and the first spatters of rain began to pelt the slickrock. "Helping someone is a virtue too," Rick said. "Hey, I'm really in a jam here."

"More like a pickle sandwich," Gunderson said with a self-impressed chuckle. "Let's get going, Nuke, 'fore we get hit by lightning."

It was Carlile, obviously, who was going to make the decision. But the malevolence in his face was unalloyed with any hint of compassion. Without a word Carlile turned on his heel, and the other followed smugly. In a moment they'd disappeared.

Rick was stunned. He hadn't imagined they'd just leave him there. They knew his life was in danger. He tried desperately to climb the slick pitch—once, twice, three times. Each time he peeled off. The holds just weren't there. "Hey," he yelled, sure the men must be standing by, enjoying his predicament. "Hey! Quit fooling around!"

Not a sound came back, none at all. Rick heard nothing but the booming and rumbling of thunder. Suddenly he knew better than to think they were fooling around. This was pure malice, inexplicable but no less real.

Rocks, he had to have rocks. If he could stand on a platform even twenty inches high, he could pull himself up and out.

No rocks in sight, not a single one.

It was starting to rain hard. He ran around the corner, retrieved the spotting scope. There, very close to the edge of the cliff, were the rocks he needed. If this canyon had flash-flooded just a little stronger when it had last run, they would have been swept over the edge.

No time to lose. The rain slashed harder and harder, and the canyon floor was already starting to run a stream where none had existed moments before. He knew exactly what would happen to him if the water came roaring through here. He'd be a mouse trying to climb the walls of a hundred-foot bathtub. The water would come surging through here and flush him over the giant pour-over.

Five rocks and he had his platform. He built it to the side of the slick, funnellike chute that was spouting a waterfall where not a drop of water had run minutes before. From his platform, with a jump, he was able to plant his fingertips on a tiny shelf of rock above. With all his strength he was able to pull himself up high enough to get a toehold on the rock, and with the toehold he was able to move one hand and then the next. He pulled himself all the way up.

The canyon was running a foot deep in water. He ran along the sides where it was shallowest and raced back out. The men, the dog, and the Humvee were nowhere in sight.

The rain was easing as the storm cell moved north toward the Green River. Rick realized he was trembling, and he sat down on the slickrock. He watched the thunder cell pummel the Island in the Sky across the river. A double rainbow appeared.

All he wanted was to get back to camp, tell Lon what had happened, tell him what he knew. He got up and took off running. At Lizard Rock he retrieved the mountain bike and pedaled hard for home.

Lon listened soberly to his account. When Rick was finished, he said, "Thank goodness you had the presence of mind to hide the spotting scope. It sounds like you're right—he has no suspicions that you saw what you saw. Even so, he was willing to let nature have its way with you so he'd never have to wonder. I underestimated the evil in these men by a long shot. I was so sure they were pothunters!"

"No wonder Nuke was worried about your radios! No wonder he was so afraid of going to jail!"

"With the bombs they've made and the illegal weapons they've accumulated . . . throw in the possibility of the ranger station fire being pinned on them . . . they'd spend the rest of their lives in prison."

"Shouldn't you drive out right now and call the FBI or something?"

Lon was shaking his head. "And make him suspicious? As soon as he gets back to Hanksville he's going to be watching the road or having Gunderson watch it. If we do anything unexpected, he'll know we're on to him. When we go out six days from now, on schedule, we'll make a few phone calls, and not from Hanksville. Nothing's going to happen between now and then."

"Can I still fly tomorrow?"

"I think you should. It'll show we aren't worried. If we look worried, he's gonna feel real threatened."

20

Lon clipped his portable two-way to his belt as Rick prepared to fly the next day. "Too bad about the antenna," Lon said, "but we've got a radio and a mike. I think we can establish radio communication while you're flying. At close range, with no obstructions and you above me, we might be okay. I'd like to be able to coach you during, instead of just before and after."

Time after time Rick glided over the gentle slopes of the lower dune field and onto the landing zone. He was getting the feel of the control bar, learning quickly how responsive the wing was, flying more smoothly all the time without overcorrecting.

The two-way helped immensely. Lon was able to stand below and coach him from takeoff to landing. "You look like a natural to me," said the crackling voice in Rick's helmet as the wind held him up for a flight that lasted, according to the variometer, thirty-seven seconds. "Great sled run."

"What's that?"

"A flight that only loses altitude, never gains any."

Rick wanted much more than sled runs, but he didn't say so.

"Your second day was a triumph," Lon concluded around noon. "Let's head for home."

As they passed the Chimney Rock camp, Carlile and Gunderson were striking their tent. Rick held his breath as they passed by. With a glance he saw only the usual stares. He wondered if they were surprised to see him.

An hour later, from camp, Rick and Lon watched the Humvee drive out up the dugway. "Let that be the last of them," Lon said quietly, almost like a prayer. "That's all I ask."

On the morning of his third day trying to fly—Day Three, as he was calling it—Rick shouldered the furled glider up to the crest of the highest dune. When he looked over the edge, it felt more like he was on the top of a mountain. He was aware that fear was distorting his perceptions.

"You're looking at a hundred and fifty feet of vertical spread out over three hundred yards," Lon advised.

You wanted to do this, Rick told himself. "I'm ready for it," he said nervously. He breathed deep, hefted the glider off the ground, stared down his runway. He knew beyond a doubt that he wanted this. He wanted it badly. "Clear!" he hollered when the wind was right.

As he felt the lift and his churning legs left the ground, he knew he was off to his best effort yet. Once he was in the air, the fear was gone. The sensation of flight felt indescribably clean, beyond beautiful, and this flight was lasting far longer than any before. "You're looking good," crackled Lon's commentary through heavy static. "Push back just a little. . . ."

"I'm *feeling* good," he replied. He flew the entire length of the dunes, all the way down to the beginning of the landing zone. Little matter that he landed like a wounded duck.

"You're ready to start working on turns," Lon announced.

On Rick's next flight he banked the glider for the first time. When the horizon rocked on its axis he was sure he would plummet straight to the earth.

"Trust the glider," came Lon's voice. "It's a remarkable machine."

With the shift of his hands, the horizon returned to horizontal.

After every landing he only wanted to go again. Now he was truly flying, controlling the glider, not merely floating. He relished making the adjustments as he used the strength of his upper body to pull on the control bar, shifting his body weight to the left or the right.

On his last flight of the day he executed a 360-degree spiral en route to landing at the very end of the LZ. He'd flown nearly a mile, and his flight was no sled run. He'd pushed his body weight back from the bar, not so far as to stall the glider, just far enough to slow down and climb. He heard the sweet chirping sound of the variometer that indicated he was gaining altitude, and he could see with his own eyes the ground falling away below. The variometer recorded that he had gained 287 feet over his altitude at launch.

"Was it a thermal?" he shouted as soon as he saw

Lon. He was still flushed with adrenaline.

"It was warm air rising—the dunes really cook toward the middle of the day. But I wouldn't call it a full-fledged thermal. Hey, you climbed 287 feet—that's terrific! You're doing great! Let's call it a day. It's time for me to check in on the birds."

In camp Lon loaded the last calf into the pickup. Rick jumped in the truck. He'd avoided the birds since Maverick died, but now he was ready.

The condors were doing well. All five had full crops; they were all up and flying. They were flying noticeably higher than before, yet remaining along the red cliffs where they could take advantage of the continuous updrafts. Lon was pleased with their social interaction as they gathered into a flock before flying to their roosts. They were nibbling one another playfully. One of them, M3, was making a game of poking her bill repeatedly under the others' wings.

On Day Four the air wasn't cooperating; it was all sled runs. But Rick was able to work on landings— over and over and over, at great expense to his chest, belly, and knees. Late morning they were alarmed by the sound of a vehicle coming down the road to the Doll House. It turned out to be some day hikers in a Jeep, and they drove out several hours later.

In the evening Rick wanted to go up the dugway again with Lon to observe the condors. Afterward, from the edge of the cliffs, they watched the sunset turn the high cirrus clouds iridescent with all the colors in an abalone shell. Rick was picturing running off the cliff and taking flight. He thought he could do it. He let his mind go. In a few minutes he was almost as high as the abalone clouds. He could feel the control bar just as certainly as if it were in his hands. He was feeling the sensation of lift, and he was visualizing all his moves.

He needed to work on carrying more speed into his landings. He'd been de-proning—untucking his feet from the bag and hanging with his legs down—a few seconds before he should have. When he did that he slowed down too quickly and fell like a ton of bricks. Or else he'd de-prone at the right time but fail to flare the nose of the glider correctly. When that happened he ended up running and crashing nose first, dragging his chest and knees. He needed to flare the glider at the right moment to produce a stall and a gentle touchdown.

Back in camp Lon brought out a small AM-FM. "Works great after dark. I want to find a weather report. High cirrus clouds can signal a front a few days off."

Lon dialed past stations playing music, a talk show in Los Angeles, a news broadcast from Oklahoma. A station from Phoenix identified itself during a break. "Let's stick with this one," Lon said. "This time of year their weather becomes ours pretty often. Arizona's on the path for moisture out of Mexico."

Within minutes they heard a brief weather report, which ended with news that had Lon leaning forward to catch every word: "A Pacific hurricane is punishing the coast of Baja California. Pandora's storm track, once she moves inland, is yet to be determined."

"Aha," Lon said. "The cirrus clouds we saw today were spin-offs from Pandora. Let's hope the storm steers east toward Texas instead of north toward Utah, so you can fly. October is infamous for floods. The worst floods on record in the Southwest were in the first half of October."

There were puffy cumulus clouds building in the distance as they drove to the dunes for Day Five. Rick was afraid Lon would say the weather was too unstable.

"Still good," Lon announced. "Still okay. Hey, remind me to fill up the tank when we get back to camp. I didn't realize I was this low on gas."

The wind was strong but not too strong. Rick made another breakthrough. He flew a series of spiraling revolutions up the warm air rising above the dune field. With his gloved left thumb, he hit the talk button. "Is this a thermal?" he called.

He could see Lon way down there standing beside the pickup. "Weak one," came the voice from below. For some reason Lon didn't seem nearly as excited as he should have been. Why was that?

On his last flight of the morning Rick knew he was gaining the most altitude yet. He spiraled up, up, while continuously glancing below. He wondered if Lon was going to let him keep climbing.

Simultaneously he heard Lon's voice in the helmet and saw him beckoning. "Come down, Icarus."

Rick thumbed the mike. "Hey, don't call me Icarus."

"Come down and I won't have to."

For a moment he thought about continuing his climb. He had the strength to fight the turbulence he was beginning to feel.

The man's voice crackled again, this time with more anxiety: "Back to earth, Maverick."

"Name's Rick," he replied. "Not Mav-rick. Ten-four, Daedalus, I'm coming back to earth."

The most important thing now was to get down safely. He was up so high the landing was going to be more difficult than any he'd made before. The streamers down on the landing zone indicated that the wind had shifted direction and was blowing from the west. Lon had predicted it would. He knew what he would have to do—fly east with the wind, almost the length of the landing zone, nosing the glider gradually down all the while. Then he'd make his turn, a hundred or so feet above the ground, and land directly into the wind, to the west.

With his heart in his throat, he pulled it off. He landed without even going down on his knee pads.

"Born to fly!" he hollered as he reached around to unhook. He knelt down and punched in the altitude check on the variometer. His high point had been 368 feet above his takeoff altitude.

"Incredible!" Lon declared, grabbing Rick and throwing his arm around him. "You're a natural! Must be all those years of practicing in your sleep."

"Did you see the way I nailed the landing?" He was still sky-high.

"I saw, I saw. It's almost scary how fast you're picking this up, Rick. I was a hang gliding instructor years ago. I only saw one guy pick it up this fast. It should have taken you more like eight or ten days to get to this point instead of five."

"So when do I get to jump off the cliff?" Rick asked, adding quickly, "Just kidding."

"Well," Lon said, "let's see . . . you still have a few more days. Josh is coming in the day after tomorrow."

"The evening of Day Seven."

"If the weather allows you to fly tomorrow morning, and it goes well, then I'd say you'd be ready for a sled run off the cliffs on your last day. Strictly a sled run while dropping eight hundred feet. No climbing."

"Are you serious? The cliffs?"

"I never joke about hang gliding."

"You don't have to worry about it. No way I'm going to jump off those cliffs!"

As soon as he'd said it, he knew it was exactly what he wanted, if he could only overcome the fear.

The day ended badly. An hour before sunset they saw the Humvee returning down the dugway. Before it got dark, Rick scrambled to the top of a boulder with the binoculars. "They've set up their camp again," he reported. "They're definitely back."

Lon was shaking his head. "Like malaria," he said ominously. "I thought we'd seen the last of them. These guys are starting to get a little tiresome."

"Can we still fly tomorrow?"

"Weather permitting."

They tuned in the AM-FM. It was raining hard in Phoenix. "It's a slow-moving system," the forecaster was saying. "Still tracking to the north."

The morning sky was ribbed with orange cirrus. "Still a go," Lon advised.

At the dunes Lon was getting worried about the wind. "Starting to kick up in advance of the storm," he said slowly. "It's right on the cusp of being too windy, but still okay."

Rick was eager to use the wind to his advantage. He had the feeling this was going to be his last day in the air, as well as one of his last days of freedom. He made four flights and gained altitude on every one. On his last he recorded a personal best, gaining 412 feet.

Midafternoon, back in camp, they were sharing a box of cookies and watching the condors soar the rim above camp. Suddenly one of the birds broke away from the cliffs, as Maverick had.

Rick saw the condor look down at them, saw the bird flap its broad wings once, twice, and he heard the condor music from its long, extended primaries as it passed directly above.

Lon lunged for his radio and identified the bird with the first frequency he tried. "M1," he muttered.

"Keep your eye on that bird," Lon ordered as he snatched up his binoculars and sprinted toward the truck. "Where is she?" he called as he clambered atop the cab with his binoculars.

"Standing Rocks. Right now she's above the Wall."

In a minute the condor was a tiny speck to Rick, and then he lost it. He said nothing to distract Lon, who was still locked on to the bird.

"Landed on top of Chimney Rock," Lon announced finally.

"Carlile!" Rick cried.

"Bad luck. Quick, grab the two-way radio, stuff it in my daypack, where Carlile won't see it. At close range it could still help me locate that bird. My daypack's hanging up in my tent. Stuff my fleece jacket in there while you're at it. I'll get the net. Let's see, a pack of hot dogs, some water, bird kennel . . ."

Rick sprinted for Lon's tent. The daypack wasn't that big to begin with, and it already contained Lon's red rain suit, a first-aid kit, and a flashlight.

"Hurry!" Lon yelled.

21

Rick had been moving so fast, he realized he'd packed the two-way down in the bottom of the daypack with the mike and its cord still jacked in. Lon wasn't going to be talking with the condor, just tracking it.

Lon came running into the tent. He rummaged through the top drawer of his dresser, and his hand came out with the sheath knife. He paused only long enough to feed it onto his belt.

"What's that for?"

"The dog, if need be. Let's go!"

Halfway to Chimney Rock they heard the crack of a high-powered rifle, then its echoing report.

The man who loved the condors pounded the steering wheel with his fist. "Now he's done it . . . now he's done it!"

Lon drove fast into the campsite and braked hard, stepped out in a cloud of red dust. The pit bull was growling, while Carlile was commanding it to stay at his side.

Rick couldn't see the body of the bird anywhere. It could have fallen on the other side of Chimney Rock, he realized. His eyes returned to Carlile and his partner. From the taunting, aggressive look on Gunderson's face, Rick guessed that he was the one who had done the shooting.

"Where's the bird?" Lon demanded.

Carlile cleared his throat. "Ain't seen a bird."

"Rick," Lon instructed, "run over there and look around the other side of the formation."

Rick took off running. Five minutes later he was back shaking his head.

"The gunshot," Lon demanded. "Explain the gunshot."

"Shoulda asked in the first place," Carlile huffed. "Is target shooting illegal all of a sudden?"

"In a national park it is."

Nuke spit on the ground. "I'm not surprised."

Gunderson was about to say something. Nuke cut him off with an abrupt gesture. Carlile's eyes were on the big sheath knife at the biologist's hip. "We haven't seen one of your precious vultures. Now, why don't you leave us be?"

Abruptly Lon strode back to the truck. He snatched his daypack from the seat, slung it on his back, lifted the fiberglass kennel cage and then the big net from the back of the camper shell. "Rick," he called, motioning with a wave of his head.

Lon put the truck keys in Rick's hand.

"Lon," Rick protested, but the man was shaking his head.

"I'm not going down in any canyons, I promise you," Lon said, loud enough to be overheard. "The bird will be up on the rims or ridges. She'd be afraid of flying down into those narrow canyons."

"Lon," Rick whispered urgently, facing the truck. "Let's stick together. I have a bad feeling."

Lon turned his back on the two men as well. "I need you to watch camp. I don't know what to expect from these guys."

"Exactly. Forget M1, Lon."

"I can't," the biologist insisted. "I'd be down to four. Every condor is too essential, you know that. I've got a fair chance of netting her if I can locate her. She'll stay up high, Rick, like I was saying; odds are she's not that far away. I need to recapture them all and pen them until it's resolved with these guys. I promise I'll be back before dark."

"And if you're not?"

"An hour after dark, get in the truck and drive. Drive to a pay phone. Get Josh at Cliff Dweller's Lodge, Vermilion Cliffs, Arizona—number's in the glove box. He's due here tomorrow night—he'll still be there until tomorrow morning. Tell him everything you know. Tell him I need help. He'll know what to do."

"What if those guys come into camp this afternoon?"

"Keep your daypack ready with some food and water. Don't let them get close to you. Run, hide in the Maze."

"This is crazy. You don't even have a gun."

"They don't want to shoot me."

"No, they'll use the dog."

"No, they won't. Carlile saw the knife. He doesn't want to lose that dog."

"Don't . . ." Rick pleaded. "They might still be moving their stuff."

"Then they can wait for me to clear out. I won't go anywhere near that cave you told me about. They won't feel threatened."

Exasperation filled Lon's eyes. "Gotta go," he said, his hand briefly to Rick's shoulder. "But I want to see you driving out of here before I take off. And don't forget to fill up when you get back to camp—we're nearly running on empty. Good luck to us both!"

Rick tried to pump gas from the big fuel drum on stilts. Nothing, not a drop. What could possibly be wrong? There was nothing complicated about it. It was a simple gravity feed, and he'd done it before.

He rapped his knuckles on the tank. It sounded hollow as a drum. He leaned his shoulder to the stand and pushed with one hand. He could have tipped the drum over.

Empty. The realization made him go light-headed. When had they stolen the gas? That morning, when he and Lon were at the dunes?

His stomach went queasy. They were stranded. No possibility of calling in help, no way to escape. There could be no doubt that Carlile and Gunderson had returned for more of their contraband. And they didn't want to take the slightest chance.

Should he take the bicycle and go for help? Sixty miles, that was how far he'd have to ride. Lon had told him to wait until an hour after dark, but that was assuming he had the truck. How long would it take him to bicycle sixty miles? Forever. Out in the open like that, the Humvee would catch him and squash him like a bug. "Hide in the Maze"—that was what Lon had said.

It was excruciating, waiting for Lon's return. It was

the longest day of his life. Unmindful that everything was going horribly wrong, the four condors soared back and forth above the red cliffs. The cumulus clouds boiled up tall and massive, turned dark, and began to rumble—forerunners of the hurricane moisture that was on its way. All the while Rick kept scanning the slickrock canyon rims to the east with the spotting scope. No glimpse of Lon returning. Nothing.

Every minute, every second, he listened for the Humvee. He couldn't guess what they were going to do next, but it might involve him. They might even try to sneak up on him on foot.

Rick's daypack was stuffed full with everything he might need, including maps and a compass, and he was keeping it within arm's length. He was ready to bolt for the Maze.

It rained. It rained hard enough to drown a cat.

At first the downpour agitated him, and then it terrified him. *Lon, you better not be down in a place like I was.*

After ten minutes the rain quit.

Nothing to do but wait. It was 3:00 P.M., 4:00 P.M., 5:00 P.M. Across the Colorado, from north to south and everywhere but above the Maze, thunderheads were spitting lightning and spilling rain that was dark and dense as a wall. He could imagine all too well the flash floods that were sluicing through thousands of canyons.

Then he heard a distant gunshot. Moments later, its echo. The sound had come from the east, from the direction of Jasper Canyon.

He knew what it meant. They'd killed him.

A second shot was followed quickly by a third, and a fourth and a fifth. Rick closed his eyes.

Then only the sound of unraveling thunder. He tried to think of a reason for hope, and he found it in the number of shots. There was virtually no cover where Lon had gone. One shot should have been enough if they were trying to kill him. Maybe they were driving him away from their cave. But no, Lon knew not to go near the cave. Maybe they had a whole other cache of weapons, somewhere different, and Lon had gotten too close to it. . . .

The shots could mean anything. Those men were capable of anything. His skin tingled and the hair rose on the back of his neck. If Lon was dead, they'd come for him next.

The gunshots changed everything. He couldn't wait helplessly in camp. He had to do something. It had to be something they'd never expect.

They'd never expect him to come to them. On foot he could do that. There was plenty of cover to take advantage of along the way. At their camp he would have a chance of finding out what had happened and what they'd do next.

Rick started out, keeping the Maze close on his left, the road on his right. He could be down in the Maze in a minute if he had to run for it.

He went so slowly, used his cover so carefully that dusk gathered while he was still under way. He was grateful for the twilight. He could move a little more quickly. The moon, half full, appeared to be racing through the clouds.

At last he was approaching Chimney Rock's tall silhouette. At some moments the moon was ghostly pale behind the clouds; seconds later it was shining bright and lighting up the monolith.

He could hear the two even before he saw the

bright white light cast by their propane lantern. Their voices were bitter. Arguments were flying back and forth. "How could you be so stupid!" Carlile fumed.

"How was I supposed to know the guy would go off chasing the bird?"

"You shoulda never fired that shot in the first place. That's what brought him over here. Or you could have shot to kill and been done with it. But shooting at the bird just to scare it—idiotic. You just didn't *think*. The bird might fly toward our cache, the guy might follow. . . . It wouldn't have taken a rocket scientist, Gunderson."

Rick stepped cautiously, approached closer, and crouched behind a juniper. Through the branches he could see them clearly. Carlile was seated on a lawn chair with his back to Rick. The dog was at his side. Gunderson was pacing back and forth with arms folded. "So, what's the big problem?" Gunderson exploded.

"The problem is, because of you, we haven't been able to do what we came here for. We just wasted the whole afternoon following that bird guy while he blundered closer and closer to our second cache."

I was right, Rick realized. They do have a second hiding place, more weapons.

"You're the one who started shooting at him, Nuke. Quit tryin' to blame it all on me."

"I had to scare him away from the cave—he was looking right at our stuff."

"You don't know he saw anything. He had his binoculars on the *bird*, not on the cave. The bird was on the rim. Why would he have been focusing on the cave, through the brush and all, when the bird was in plain sight on the rim?"

"Okay, maybe he wasn't looking at the cave. I just

don't like it. Too much slop. That's the way it is with you, Gunderson. All slop and no discipline."

"Hey, I told you we shouldn't put both caches in the same canyon. That was your bright idea, putting everything in Jasper. Look, Nuke, where that guy is stuck—"

"You don't *know* he's stuck, you just *think* he's stuck. He might be out of there already."

Lon's alive, Rick realized.

"What are the chances?" Gunderson thundered. "Look, he's trapped below one of those ledges down in that side canyon. You saw where he jumped when you fired those shots. He can't get back up, so the only way he can go is down, and he won't get far that way. That big storm is supposed to be here tomorrow, and when that hits, he's gonna be history."

Carlile was furious. "You idiot. You still don't get it. The whole place is going to be crawling with search and rescue."

"So? What are the chances, out of all that country out there, they'd look in that one cave? They'll find a dead body down in the canyon, call off this vulture project, and we come back later and get our stuff. No problem."

"And what about the kid? We don't know for sure that he didn't see something last week."

"Ninety-nine out of a hundred, he didn't."

"That's not good enough."

Rick went from his crouch down onto one knee, to ease his back. The dog must have heard something. The pit bull growled, lifted its ears.

"Shut up, Jasper!" Carlile rasped, and gave the dog a kick.

"What do you want to do now, Nuke?"

"We don't have much choice. With this storm coming, we clear out of here in the morning. Empty-handed, thanks to you. We could have had every-thing out of here, neat and tidy, been done with it. Now everything's slop, all slop."

Rick backed away and started for camp. He was hoping against hope that Lon would be waiting there when he got back.

Lon wasn't there. He must be trapped, just like Gunderson said.

Rick was afraid to sleep in his tent; Carlile might come for him. He took a sleeping bag into a cleft in the rocks nearby, where he could keep an eye out. The moon set, and the stars shone only intermittently, but even in the near darkness he could have made out a silhouette moving in camp. If only it would be Lon. He saw no one. Lightning lit the horizon like monumental strobe lights.

He followed the weather reports from Salt Lake City on the AM-FM. The station was predicting heavy weather for the coming afternoon, with flash flood watches likely to be upgraded to flash flood warnings. "Pandora is no longer a hurricane, but she's packing a tremendous wallop tonight in parts of Arizona and New Mexico," the forecaster said. "The eastern half of southern Utah and the western half of southern Colorado are in for a pounding."

An idea like a flickering candle of hope kept appearing in the back of Rick's mind. Every time he extinguished it, it returned. It was too far-fetched, too impossible to be considered.

Or was it?

He couldn't search on the ground, he knew that. Jasper had dozens of side canyons on each side, and it was ten miles long. Trapped in one of those narrow slots, Lon would be impossible to spot from the rim.

His idea burned brighter and brighter, yet he was scared to death of it. He was afraid he was getting crazy from fear, crazy from desperation. Still he knew, he *knew* there was a way to get to Lon if he had the courage.

22

Forty feet away, at the edge of the cliff, the wind was snapping the green streamer. It was early morning. At the margins of the canyonlands, the clouds were already boiling up and erasing the blue of the sky. Yet inside him there was a strange calm.

Methodically, Rick arranged the thin metal ribs along the rear of the wing, and then he knelt and slipped them one by one into their sleeves. He fastened the guy wires to the king post that stood vertically above the wing.

He was going to do this thing. He couldn't live with not trying.

There was reason to try. Lon would be wearing the bright red rain suit, for visibility. Lon would think he'd driven out and called for help—he'd be looking to the sky, hoping against hope for a search plane or a helicopter.

If he couldn't spot Lon, surely Lon would see the hang glider up above him. And Lon had the two-way. If he was up above Lon, the radio should work.

It all sounded plausible, but it depended on him getting up in the air above Jasper Canyon. This had to be more than a sled run. If he didn't gain altitude, he couldn't fly as far as Jasper Canyon. He had to catch a thermal.

Was he crazy to think he could do that?

From the tandem flight they'd made together, he could remember the turbulence inside a thermal all too vividly. He didn't know if he could control the glider in that kind of turbulence, but he should be strong enough. He thought he could. And if he thought he could, he had to try.

He was fitting the fabric cover over the nose of the glider and fastening its closures when the sound of a motor, extremely close, startled him. He looked up. It was the Humvee coming over the top of the dugway.

Nuke Carlile drove no more than a hundred feet onto the plateau, then slowed to a stop and took a long look. Rick knew better than to appeal to him. It would waste time he didn't have. Just leave me alone, he thought. Quickly he fitted one of the small plastic wheels and then the other to the ends of the control bar.

He heard the Humvee starting away toward Hanksville. He wouldn't look at it go. He walked around the wing twice. Everything looked right.

Rick took the long climbing rope that he'd found in Lon's tent and fitted it into the compartment at the back of the harness. He tucked Maverick's flight feather inside for good luck and zippered the pouch closed. Stepping with one leg and then the other into the harness, he drew on the shoulder straps.

Suddenly, in his imagination, the axis of the earth was tilting, and he was swimming in unreality. The horizon went spinning. He recalled the phrase *tuck and tumble.*

He fought the panic back by focusing on what he was doing. He fastened his cocoon from belly to neck, buckled the parachute compartment across his chest. Almost certainly he was going to have to land on stone, on the slickrock terraces above Jasper. He'd never landed on stone before. He blew out a big breath and reached for the helmet.

"Hook in," Rick said aloud as he reached over his shoulder for the carabiner gathering his harness lines. He hooked the carabiner to the small loop suspended from the keel above, then swiveled the locking mechanism shut. He pulled on his gloves and jacked the radio wire at his shoulder into his helmet. He was set.

Poking his helmeted head underneath the peak where the downtubes met the keel, he reached around the tubes, grasped them, and lifted. He walked the glider ten feet forward, set it back down.

Thirty feet from the edge of infinity, that was where he stood. His heart was trying to bludgeon its way out of his chest. His stomach swooned as his eyes took in the floor of the open country far below the cliffs. Don't look down, he reminded himself.

The streamer needed to be blowing directly at him. For a few moments it did, and then it blew again from the south.

A cloud blocked the sun. He shivered and shook, and not from cold. From his right came the first rumble of approaching thunder. It was all dark over there in his peripheral vision.

He couldn't look directly above him now because

he was standing under the center of the wing, but to the northeast, the direction he needed to fly, there were still patches of blue among the clouds. He knew he had a window, but the window was shrinking fast.

It was hard to tell because of the muffling effect of his helmet, but he thought he heard a motor. Probably thunder, he thought, as he ducked his head and looked behind him under the wing.

It was the Humvee again, coming in his direction across the slickrock. He saw it crush a small juniper under its wheels.

Carlile had never left. At a distance, he'd been watching all this time.

The Humvee halted abruptly several hundred feet away. The two men got out. The dog got out.

What did Carlile want? He wasn't calling or waving. His features, as ever, were contorted by malice.

Rick had a sudden insight. He could feel it up and down his spine. Carlile meant to solve all his problems at once: no survivors.

Rick glanced back to the cliff edge and the streamer. The wind was blowing hard enough, but still from the side. He needed it to shift, and soon.

He looked over his shoulder again, saw the moment it happened. The command must have been spoken softly. The dog shot toward him like an arrow from a bow.

Rick's eyes found the streamer. It was blowing directly toward him. He lifted the glider and began to jog.

The cliff edge seemed to be rushing forward to meet him. He felt the tail end of his harness bag flapping at his ankles, which was normal. But he also heard the dog snarling close behind, much too close.

Suddenly he felt the powerful lift of the wing, and his pedaling feet found only air. As the glider soared out over empty space, he shifted his hands quickly to the control bar.

Something was wrong. A dead weight at the bottom of his harness bag was keeping him from assuming a prone position. With a glance below he saw the pit bull hanging on by its powerful jaws.

He couldn't do anything about that. All he could do was try to fly the glider. The variometer's buzzing warned him that he was falling. Flying with his legs down, plus the weight of the dog, was causing him to sink.

He couldn't worry about that. All he could do was try to keep the wing stable. He couldn't afford to let either wing tip get up in the air on him.

The dog might have tried for a better grip, opened its jaws for a fatal split second. All Rick knew was that the pull at the bottom of the bag was suddenly gone. As he looked down he saw the dog hurtling toward oblivion like a missile.

23

Rick reached with his right leg, found the bottom of the bag. He reached with his left; they were both inside. Freeing his hand for a second, he pulled the draw cord that zipped the bag shut along his legs.

Now he was prone. Now he could try to fly. He pushed himself back from the bar a little to see if the glider would climb. Immediately the variometer chirped its climbing signal. He was rising on the warm air sweeping up the face of the cliffs.

With careful shifting of his weight, he raised the right wing tip and began negotiating a turn. The glider responded, the earth turned on its axis, and he spiraled up past the rim of the cliffs, regaining the altitude he had lost. He caught a glimpse of the Humvee heading across the plateau back to Hanksville. Good riddance, he thought.

After five rising revolutions he was satisfied that he was high enough above the cliffs to glide away from them and head for Jasper Canyon.

You're still alive, he told himself as he broke to the east and began to soar toward the Standing Rocks. A powerful wave of exhilaration washed over him. He suddenly realized he was whooping and shouting like a wild man, grinning from ear to ear. "Yes!" he was screaming. "Yes!"

On his left and below, a very large bird was flying in his direction. As it neared he saw the broad wings, the distinctive wing tips, the featherless gray head. Lon's missing condor, he realized. It was M1, returning home in advance of the storm.

A glance at the variometer told him he had risen from 6,200 feet at launch to 7,560. Concentrate, he told himself. Stay focused. Take a deep breath. This is just the beginning.

Over the Standing Rocks the glider took a powerful buffeting. He clung tight as the wing shuddered with the turbulence. The variometer kept chirping as the glider was rocked by more and more turbulence. Still, he pushed back slightly from the bar and kept rising. He needed altitude. It was taking all his strength to hang on to the control bar and fly the glider. He knew now for certain that he was inside a thermal, a very powerful thermal.

Rick saw the earth's spinning, dizzying retreat below him, and he fought the panic that accompanied his sudden loss of equilibrium.

Keep fighting, he told himself. Keep flying it. Don't let it get away from you.

He didn't know if he was strong enough to keep the wing tips down. One or the other kept threatening to go too high on him. He kept yanking hard on the side he wanted to bring down.

Ride it! Fight it!

Up, up, up he went, on an increasingly powerful column of rising air. He checked the variometer. He was at eleven thousand feet and climbing at a rate of a thousand feet per minute.

Eleven thousand feet!

It was getting cold. His face was cold, his teeth were cold.

High enough! There was a river below, but he couldn't tell which one. It was all a sickening blur.

He had to break out, find Jasper Canyon.

Rick pulled his weight over the bar, but the variometer kept chirping. A glance told him he was rising now at a rate of eighteen hundred feet per minute.

The turbulence was getting worse, much worse.

Ride it! Fight it!

He heard the snap of lightning, and some time later, the unraveling thunder. How long was the interval—ten seconds? The storm was only ten miles away, and closing in how fast?

Twelve thousand, thirteen thousand, fourteen thousand feet. It was becoming nearly impossible to hang on to the bar and keep the wings down. He didn't know how much longer he could hang on. He had to start thinking about the parachute.

Icarus, he thought ruefully. I'm pulling an Icarus. "Wasn't ready to fly a thermal," Lon had said.

Sixteen thousand feet. It was cold, cold, and getting harder to breathe.

From the variometer he glanced up and saw the base of a massive cumulus cloud not so far above. He could picture exactly what was going to happen, and soon. He was going to be inside that cloud and unable to tell up from down. Tucking and tumbling.

This is the way I'm going to die.

Wildly he forced his body as far forward of the control bar as he possibly could. He spread his hands wide and held on with all his strength.

Finally, finally, the glider nosed down. He heard the buzzing that told him he was losing altitude.

He kept his body forward of the bar, kept fighting the glider down. It felt like he was dropping fast, fast.

Suddenly the nose dived much more steeply than he wanted it to, and his stomach went into free fall. He pushed his body back, but not too far back. More than anything he didn't want to stall the glider.

Abruptly he found himself in relatively stable air, and realized what had happened. He'd just gone over the falls, and was free of the thermal.

With a look around, he knew he didn't have much time. On all sides the clouds were darkening and the altitude of cloudbase was descending fast. He could see the two great rivers joining below the Island in the Sky. He could see the Maze incised into the sea of white slickrock, and he could see red-walled Jasper Canyon making its straight run from Chimney Rock to the Green River.

Rick began his downward revolutions. He'd lost three thousand feet when the variometer began to chirp again. Another thermal, he realized, and he fought his way free of it before it could take him. He continued down, steering toward the midpoint of Jasper Canyon.

He was looking hard up and down the drainage for a tiny patch of red, desperate to spot Lon's rain suit. So many side canyons! So many places Lon could be!

Rick hit the mike button on his glove with his thumb.
"Lon," he called. "Do you read me? Lon, can you hear
me? *Do you read me? Over . . .*"

Nothing.

His eyes kept searching for a tiny patch of red, arti-
ficially bright red. No matter how hard he willed it, it
just wasn't there.

He was still too high up. *Get closer.* You have to get
closer before you can see anything. Before he can see
you. Before the two-way can work.

Ten thousand feet. Nine thousand.

"*Lon, do you read me. This is Rick! This is Rick.
Look up, look up! Do you read? Over . . .*"

No reply.

Suddenly there it was, directly below and slightly
in motion: a tiny spot of artificial red. There, on the
slick floor of an extremely narrow side finger of
Jasper, on Jasper's west side. "*Condor-man!*" he cried.
"*Lon, look up, look up! This is Rick, this is Mav-rick,
this is Icarus! Over . . .*"

Suddenly the earpiece in his helmet crackled, and
crackled again. "*Get down, Icarus!*" came Lon's voice
through heavy interference. "*Storm's about to break!
Over . . .*"

"*Got you spotted! Over . . .*"

"*Save yourself, Rick!*"

His glide had taken him quickly out of eye contact.
Suddenly Rick couldn't identify the side canyon
where Lon was trapped. He circled back, losing altitude all the while. The weather was about to break.
Lightning exploded close by, and thunder boomed
seconds later with a concussive blast.

There was Lon, waving for all he was worth.

Rick studied the shape of the terraces above the

rim. Lon was a couple hundred feet below the rim, caught between two pour-overs in the northernmost of two huge side canyons that joined before draining into Jasper. At the rim of Lon's canyon there was a distinctive triangle of three junipers growing out of the slickrock, with a knob of redrock close by that was surrounded by white.

The rain broke. He was going to have to get down in the rain.

The rain, at a slant, was driving from the south. At least it made reading the wind direction easy. He had to land into the rain, from north to south.

It was getting dark, so dark. The sky above was nothing but a mass of storm cloud. He had his eye on a broad white terrace only a few hundred yards north of the side finger where Lon was trapped. How level was that terrace? He pushed his weight over the bar and forced the glider down, down, flying to the north.

Rick made his turn into the wind, the way Lon had taught him. He remembered to pull the draw cord to open the bottom of his harness so he could free his legs when the time came to de-prone.

It was starting to rain harder, but he could still make out the flat white expanse ahead.

He might overshoot his landing zone, he realized, unless he got down fast. He forced his weight far forward over the bar, then eased back a little.

The ground was rushing up. He kicked his legs free, then slid his hands from the control bar to the tubes above. He was hanging vertically now, no more than forty feet above the ground. He slid his hands farther up the tubes, but not so high as to stall the glider just yet.

Now! he decided, and he flared the nose up, felt the stall.

As his legs touched down, he was in perfect position, but a violent gust of wind lifted the right side of the wing as he was running and pitched the nose in an instant down to the slickrock. He heard the chinpiece of his helmet dragging as he scraped to a stop on his chest.

He couldn't breathe. He didn't think he'd broken any bones, but the breath was knocked out of him. His lungs couldn't draw air.

The wind was dragging the glider across the slickrock, and him with it. He was powerless to do anything about it. The rain was pelting him, lashing his face. He lay on his belly, gasping for air.

At last, in painful gasps, his breath was coming back. He was able to turn on his side and unhook.

He stood up, he fell down, he got up again. It was difficult to see, but he could make out the three junipers and the mound of redrock. He was where he'd wanted to be. But something *was* broken, he realized. His left arm was hanging useless by his side. He wasn't feeling pain for some strange reason, but he could see it was broken.

The side canyon drained an enormous area of slickrock. Waterfalls were pouring into it from all sides and running red. He had to hurry. Time was everything.

He fought his way out of the harness bag. Struggling one-handed, he removed the coil of rope from the compartment in the back.

Rick heard the glider behind him being swept away over the cliffs, but he didn't turn to look. With his good arm he slung the coil of rope over his head and onto his shoulder. He started down into the side canyon. Lon was a ways down in there, hemmed in by the walls. The only route to get to him was going to be right down the bottom of the drainage.

Where possible, Rick kept away from the streaming floor of the narrowing canyon and skittered along its stony flanks. But he kept getting cliffed out, and was forced to wade from one side to another. It was difficult to keep his balance, yet he had to move fast. The water was up to his knees and rising. He marveled that his arm wasn't screaming out in pain, but still he felt nothing.

The tumult of rushing water was intensifying behind him and above and in front. "Lon!" he hollered. *"Lon! Lon!"*

No answer. He looked up through the slashing rain; he could still see the rims. Lon would have gone farther down this canyon to find cover if they were shooting at him from above.

Up ahead the current raced through a boulder jam and down onto a steepening raceway of slickrock. Then it bent away and out of sight.

Rick wedged his way down through the boulders, then lost his footing immediately below, fell backward. He'd fallen on the broken arm. Sudden, piercing pain shot through the arm as the current swept him straight down the chute and into a roiling pool.

He was spun around and around, and then he was washed out onto the shallows. He struggled to his feet.

Lightning seared the sky immediately above him, and the thunder struck like a bomb going off. It was starting to hail. *"Lon!"* he screamed as he waded forward toward a boulder jam at the edge of the next drop.

"*Riiiiiick* . . ." came the voice in reply.

He clambered onto the boulders and looked down. Ten feet below, right there on a lip of rock to the side of the pool below the waterfall, stood the man with the beard, dressed in bright red. "A rope!" Lon shouted, with a grin spreading across his face. "You even brought a rope! Can you tie to those big rocks up there?"

"Ten-Four," Rick yelled back through the rain. He waded upstream, looking for the right boulder. The water was thigh-deep and swift; he had to keep fighting for balance.

Here was the boulder he needed. Using one hand and his teeth, he struggled to brace himself and secure the rope. It was taking much too long, and all the while he heard nothing from below, only the roar of the floodwater. Was Lon still okay? Finally his knot was tied, and he was able to toss the free end down.

Rick saw the hands appear first, then the arms, then the fierce blue eyes, the hard white scar, and the tangle of beard. Rick jammed a foot against a rock for balance and offered his good arm. Lon took it, then came on over the top, and they both followed the rope to where it was tied.

"Do we need the rope?" Rick yelled. The fingers of his right hand were picking at the knot, but he was getting nowhere with it.

Lon's eyes went to Rick's useless left arm. "We might!" he hollered back, and quickly undid the knot. Lon coiled the rope as fast as he could and slung the coil over his head. "Let's go!"

It was still raining hard. Everything ran together, the rising water and the pain and the rock walls. At one point Rick was swept from his feet. Lon leaped after him and scooped him up. Half a minute later Rick slipped again; it felt like all the strength had drained out of him. He felt Lon's grasp. "Right arm around my shoulder," he heard his friend say.

Rick felt Lon's arm clutch his side like a band of steel. He felt new strength in his legs and new determination. "Gotta go for it—let's march!" Lon shouted, and they started out side by side.

It was all a blur. At last, stumbling, they climbed out of the flooding canyon bottom onto the slickrock. In the pouring rain it was as slick as its name. Rick looked up; it was going to be a steep climb, a hundred feet or so, to the rim. Lon stopped, freed one end of the rope, and tied it around Rick's waist. "Just in case," Lon said.

The rope helped. Lon short-roped him up the steepest pitch, and at last they scuttled into a shallow cave tucked under the rimrock.

They slumped against the wall and heaved for breath. Lightning struck again and again. Through a curtain of water an arm's length away, they watched the deluge coursing below. Where they'd been just minutes before had become unthinkably impassable.

"Big-time flood," Lon said. "Big time. Not a moment too soon, Rick. I've never seen such a sight in my life, you up there flying that kite."

"I think your hang glider's history, Lon."

"But you aren't, thank God. Where did you start from?"

"Condor Cliffs, above camp."

"That was no sled run. How did you know you could do that?"

"Thought I could. Needed to do it. I knew it was dicey, but I couldn't get out to call Josh. On account of Carlile."

Suddenly he was in agony with his left arm. It must have showed on his face.

"Josh is due tonight," Lon said, "unless the storm delays him. I've got some serious pain medicine here in my pack, in my first aid. We'll find something to splint your arm with as soon as the rain slows down a little. What about Carlile? Are we going to run into them?"

"They went out."

"They've got a second cache."

"I know. Did you see it?"

"Only glassed it for a few seconds, but yeah, I saw some metal boxes. They started shooting at me. I had no choice but to run where I did. You see my bird by any chance?"

"Sure did. I think you'll find her back home with the others."

It was nearly dark when they struggled into camp. It was still raining. Lon counted five condors up on the rim. The rain was exciting them into a joyous frenzy. They were leaping around the rim, chasing one another, spreading their wings.

"Goofballs," Lon said fondly. "There'll come a day when they start pairing up. It'll be a few years yet, but it'll happen. I can really see it—that first egg."

"A condor lays only one egg?"

"That's right. On the floor of a high cave."

Rick closed his eyes. "Won't that be something. Back in the wild and on their own."

It was nearly midnight when Josh's headlights appeared on the dugway. Rick wanted to cry for joy, but he couldn't. There was no escaping what would come next.

The truck pulled into camp at last. The rain had

quit, but lightning was still attacking the mountains to the east. A young man and a young woman got out and stepped into the light cast by the propane lantern under the tarp.

"Who's your friend?" Josh asked.

"Rick," Lon replied. "His name's Rick Walker— and he can fly like a bird."

24

"All rise," the bailiff instructed.

Holding his breath, Rick came to his feet. As before, the judge swept into the courtroom from the door on the right. His ominous black robe billowed with his passage.

"Take your seats, please," the judge said impatiently. "Let's make this expeditious."

Rick exhaled, sat down. He glanced quickly to Lon, seated to his right. Lon looked different with his hair cut and his beard trimmed, new clothes and all, but the scar was the same.

"Just do your best," the deep baritone voice whispered. "Just be yourself."

Rick nodded, then looked over his left shoulder past Janice Baker, the social worker, to Mr. B., who smiled nervously.

The judge was opening the file folder in his hands while frowning at the clock. The clock read 5:35 P.M.

Rick returned his eyes to the judge. The Honorable Samuel L. Bendix, with fingers to forehead, began to read. As yet he hadn't looked at anyone with more than a passing glance. He hadn't looked at Rick at all.

Nothing was going to be different. The judge was just as out of sorts as before. Bad luck, Rick thought, that Samuel L. Bendix hadn't died in the last six months. He was old enough.

Quit thinking like that, he told himself. He'd promised Lon he was going to stay positive.

Suddenly the judge looked up and stared over his reading glasses, directly at him. The judge didn't seem to recognize him. Rick forced a weak half smile as the judge's eyes moved past him and acknowledged the adults. Rick remembered all too well the judge's "enormous discretionary power."

"Would you identify yourselves as I call your names?" the judge said. "Mr. Lon Peregrino."

Lon raised his hand.

"And Mr. Timothy Bramwell. Thank you, gentlemen. Now I can attach faces to these documents."

"Your Honor," spoke up Janice Baker, "we would like to thank you for granting this hearing. We recognize its unusual nature."

"Unusual, indeed, this plea for no further incarceration. Escape from a detention facility is considered a major offense, Ms. Baker."

"Yes, it is, Your Honor."

The social worker said nothing further. The judge's eyes dropped to the folder in front of him, and he resumed reading. He turned a page.

Rick's hopes sank. The judge hadn't read Lon's letter beforehand, or Mr. B.'s. If the letter from the judge in Arizona had arrived that morning by overnight mail, as Janice Baker assured Lon it had, the judge obviously hadn't read that either. The judge had been hearing other cases all day, and right now he wasn't reading carefully. He only wanted to go home.

How had the judge in Arizona responded to everything Lon had proposed? Was Lon right when he thought that the judge had really listened to him?

There was supposed to be a letter from the group home in Arizona in the file too. It was supposed to have come this afternoon. What were the chances it was there?

Quit thinking like that, Rick told himself.

He told himself to think well of the judge. There must be a way.

Now he could see it. It was in the way the man's head, thin and bald and red, rose from the voluminous black robe. The judge reminded him of a condor.

"Unusual," the judge said at last. "I believe that's where we left off. The request, as I understand it, is to suspend the six weeks remaining of this young man's sentence and not to add any additional time."

His social worker stood. "Yes, Your Honor."

"You may sit down, Ms. Baker. I would like to address young Mr. Walker here."

This is it, Rick thought. He doesn't even remember me, so many people come through here.

The judge's eyes went to Rick's cast. "You've broken your arm," Samuel L. Bendix began almost conversationally.

"Yes, sir."

"How did you break it? The short version, please. Very short."

The short version? Rick wondered. This was just like before—everything this judge said threw him off-balance. "In . . . sort of a fall," he answered. Lon had told him to leave out about the flying unless he couldn't avoid it.

Rick knew he sounded nervous. He wanted to glance to Lon, for instructions or at least reassurance, but he knew the judge would hold that against him. With a grimace he realized that he'd just made a mistake. From what he'd said, the judge was assuming he'd broken his arm going over the fence at Blue Canyon.

"Who is Rick Walker?" the judge asked suddenly. Rick was off-balance again. The judge didn't remember having asked him this the first time, or did he?

It felt like there was a huge weight on him, forcing him down in the hard bench seat, as if he were being crushed. He couldn't find the words sitting down. "Can I stand up?" he asked, almost desperately. At least he was buying some time.

"You may," the judge said, seemingly amused.

As Rick stood, he was still swimming in confusion. He didn't even know what he was going to say. This was exactly how he'd felt six months before.

But that wasn't him, not anymore. If he could only stay calm, dig deep, he could explain the difference.

He *knew* the difference. Just say it, he told himself.

"Since my grandmother died," he began, "four years ago, I've been like a rat in a maze."

"Not a pretty image," the judge remarked, "but descriptive."

"Yes, sir. I was only trying to survive, and I kept running into dead ends. But I don't feel like that anymore, thanks to this man."

Rick glanced briefly to his right, caught a glimpse of the scar, looked back to the judge.

"I'm out of that maze now, sir. I'm free to make something of myself."

"If you were to be returned to detention, wouldn't you be back in the maze again?"

"Not in my *mind*."

"An excellent response," the judge said, his eyes sweeping approvingly across the courtroom. "A most excellent response. The court is aware that you were, through no merit of your own, in the position to make a certain discovery in regards to a cache or caches of illegal weaponry, ammunition, bombs, and so on, inside Canyonlands National Park during the time you were evading pursuit."

"Yes, Your Honor," Rick said quietly.

"The court is curious if you believe that cooperating with the U.S. attorney's investigation in this affair should influence the judgment of this court today?"

Rick had hoped that it would, but Lon had warned him it wouldn't. "No, Your Honor," he responded.

"You are correct in that assumption. Nevertheless, this court is grateful that you were instrumental in the apprehension of two suspects in a very serious case that could have proved extremely costly to human life."

"Thank you, sir."

"You may sit down, Mr. Walker."

Janice Baker cleared her throat. "Would it please Your Honor to hear from Mr. Peregrino and Mr. Bramwell?"

"Considering the hour, that won't be necessary. The court is impressed that Mr. Walker has acquired advocates such as these. As displeased as the court must remain in regards to young Mr. Walker's solution to his dilemma at the Blue Canyon center, the court recognizes that corruption of the sort he may have witnessed there is hardly unprecedented. Charges have recently been filed against five Blue Canyon employees in an unrelated situation. Mr. Bramwell, who has resigned his position there within the last week, has agreed to serve as one of the state's witnesses in that case."

In complete surprise, Rick looked over his shoulder to Mr. B., who wasn't wearing his usual smile. The librarian was nodding in somber agreement with the judge.

Had Mr. B. done what he had in order to strengthen one fourteen-year-old boy's position when he went back to court? Was that possible?

"Solutions," the judge intoned. "This court is interested in *solutions*. I find the package in front of me entirely acceptable. Rick Walker will be transferred to the jurisdiction of Judge Thomas Haskins of Page, Arizona. He will live in the group home in Page and will attend Page High School. His status will remain strictly probationary. Rick Walker will serve the remaining six weeks of his original sentence, plus an additional six weeks, in service to the Condor Project, either at its Arizona site or its Utah site. Mr. Lon Peregrino of the Condor Project will personally conduct the subject to Page, Arizona—"

The judge looked up, looked at Lon. "Tomorrow, as I understand it."

"Tomorrow," Lon said.

"And enroll him immediately in the group home and the high school."

The judge looked over his glasses, scanned the

faces in front of him. "Are there any further questions? No? In that case this court is no longer in session."

The judge rose and strode out of the room without looking back.

Rick went straight to Mr. B. "Thank you," he said.

Mr. B.'s large, round face broke into his good-natured smile. "You're welcome," he said. "Have a good life, Rick."

"You were a great librarian, you know."

The man shrugged. "I hope so. But it was time for me to leave."

They were passing through the outskirts of Las Vegas on the interstate. Blue Canyon was close, Rick realized, and then he sensed they'd already passed it by. With a glance over his shoulder, he caught a glimpse of the walls across a mile of flats sprinkled with creosote bushes and cut by arroyos.

He thought of the Kid Who Eats Glass. He wondered what would become of Killian.

He wondered if even Killian's parents should be forgiven. He didn't know the answer to that.

But he realized that he'd forgiven his. Can't move on until you do, he remembered. And he *had* moved on. He could feel it deep inside.

He was looking forward to living in the group home in Page, Arizona, and going to Page High School. He wasn't going to know anyone there, but he had a feeling he was going to find some friends.

Lon had his turn signal on. Up ahead the sign pointed out the road over the Hoover Dam across the Colorado. "What does Page look like?" Rick wondered aloud.

"It's surrounded by redrock," Lon replied with an

expansive sweep of his hand. "Sits on a bluff right above the Colorado River. From the high school you'll be looking west, smack at the Vermilion Cliffs beyond Glen Canyon Dam. To the north, across Lake Powell, you'll be looking into Utah. It's all drop-dead scenery. Keep your eyes open for condors—you'll be well within the range of the birds from Vermilion Cliffs."

"Tell me about those nine new condors you're supposed to get in December."

"I'll introduce you in person over Christmas break."

"Let's talk about next summer, about working together at the Maze."

"One thing . . . I can't promise you I'll have the money saved up for a new solo glider. Doubt I will—that'll run close to four thousand dollars."

"That's just as well. I've had enough of solo for the time being. What about the tandem, though?"

"Tandem it is."

AUTHOR'S NOTE

The idea for *The Maze* came as I trained a spotting scope on a juvenile condor soaring above the majestic Vermilion Cliffs near the Grand Canyon. My wife, Jean, and I were huddled there with three hardy bird biologists on a bitterly cold, windy day in late December 1996.

We'd driven from our home in southwestern Colorado hoping to catch a glimpse of this largest and rarest land bird in North America, after having read about the historic release of six fledgling condors less than two weeks before. Biologist Mark Vekasy from The Peregrine Fund explained why one of the condors was back in the release pen rather than in the air with the others. The day before, he'd had to capture the bird after a remarkable yet premature flight that ended on the flats ten miles away. There was drama here, I realized. I started thinking about putting fledgling condors together with a "fledgling boy" in a story.

The Peregrine Fund's field notes from the Vermilion Cliffs, updated several times a month on the Internet, proved invaluable as I wrote the novel. Interested readers can follow the condors' ongoing adventures via computer (http://www.peregrinefund.org). There's also an excellent National Audubon Video narrated by Robert Redford entitled *California Condor*. I'd like to extend my appreciation to all the dedicated people in the field and in the zoos who are helping bring the condor back from the brink of extinction.

I'd also like to thank three hang glider pilots from my hometown of Durango, Colorado, who gave generously of their expertise: Dennis Haley, Keith Ystesund, and Debrek Baskins. It was a thrill to watch them fly.

For the Blue Canyon section of the novel I am indebted to John Haueisen, who was a librarian for more than a decade at a juvenile detention facility. His willingness to share anecdotes and background material with me provided the true-to-life details I needed for authenticity. All the characters in my story, as well as the facility itself, are entirely fictional.

Researching the Maze on foot was pure pleasure— I've been a canyon hiker for years. For the purposes of the story I have slightly fictionalized the area. In real life the primitive road descends the cliffs five miles away from where I've placed Lon's camp. I've added the spring behind his camp and the sand dunes Rick used for a training hill. Their landing zone near the Doll House, as well as the rest of the topography of the Maze district, is as described.

I chose the edge of the Maze for the condor reintroduction base in my story for thematic purposes and for its stunning beauty. There is not an actual condor project in this location. Tantalizingly, however, one of the original six condors released in December 1996 overflew the Maze in July 1997 during an epic flight of 180 miles, soaring all the way from Vermilion Cliffs, Arizona, to the vicinity of Moab, Utah.

Durango, Colorado
December 1997